"Are you alo[ne?"](#)
lowering her v[oice]

Jay's eyebrows ros[e]
minidress, silk stoc[kings ... high heels.]
"Not any more."

"Can I come in?"

"I don't know. The last time you were here, you ran out. Told me you had to get home to your husband. You stole my hairbrush, too. Maybe I better go hide my razor before I let you in."

Susannah reached out and gently placed her palm on his chest. "I promise I won't take anything," she said. "Unless, of course, it's offered." She felt his heartbeat, slow, steady and loving, beneath her hand.

"What do you want?" he asked, steeling himself to her touch.

She smoothed her palms across his chest, feeling the hard muscle and warm flesh through his soft T-shirt. "What do *you* want?" she countered.

He reached out and touched the thin strap of her dress, skimming his knuckles along the tops of her breasts. Then he twisted a strand of her hair around his finger and pulled her closer.

"I want you..." he uttered softly.

KATE HOFFMANN
is also the author
of these novels in
Temptation

INDECENT EXPOSURE
WANTED: WIFE

LOVE POTION
No. 9

BY

KATE HOFFMANN

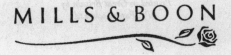

MILLS & BOON

MILLS & BOON and the Rose Device are trademarks of the publisher.
TEMPTATION is a trademark of Harlequin Enterprises Limited, used under licence.
This edition published by arrangement with Harlequin Enterprises B.V.
First published in Great Britain in 1995
by Harlequin Mills & Boon Limited, Eton House, 18-24 Paradise Road, Richmond, Surrey TW9 1SR

© Peggy Hoffmann 1994

ISBN 0 263 79041 X

21 - 9501

Printed in Great Britain by
BPC Paperbacks Ltd

1

SHE CAME OUT OF nowhere, stepping right in front of his car. Jay Beaumont slammed the brake pedal to the floor and yanked the steering wheel to the right. The sports car skidded on the snowy street before it came to a bone-jarring stop against the curb. Jay closed his eyes. His gloved hands gripped the steering wheel like a vise and his heart pumped adrenaline through his bloodstream at a dizzying rate. Taking a deep breath, he opened his eyes and looked through the windshield.

With a shudder of relief, he saw the woman step onto the curb on the other side of the street. Jay sank back into the soft leather seat. He hadn't hit her. Thank God, she was all right. As he watched her stride down the sidewalk past the business school, her nose buried in a notebook, his relief gradually gave way to anger.

Who the hell did she think she was? She hadn't even bothered to look back to see if he was all right. Hadn't bothered to acknowledge the serious damage she had wreaked on the alignment of a finely tuned European driving machine. Not to mention the jolt to his nervous system. And where the hell was he supposed to get the Jag fixed? The nearest dealer was probably in Chicago, a ninety-minute drive from the tiny college town of Riversbend.

Jay jumped out of the car and took off after her. Slipping and sliding on the snowy street, he cursed the expensive Italian shoes he wore and the early April snowstorm that had left behind more than a foot of snow. The street slush soaked through the leather in an instant. Great! He would just have to add a pair of Gucci loafers to her bill for the car.

"Hey, lady," he shouted. She didn't slow her pace or acknowledge his presence.

He was close behind her, his approach muffled by the layer of snow on the sidewalk. Matching her pace, he reached out to grab for her elbow. Suddenly she came to a dead stop. In the split second before he barreled into her, he noticed she held up a pen in an odd gesture of warning, as if asking for silence or a moment to think. A tiny yelp of surprise was the only sound she made before they both plowed into the three-foot-high snowbank beside the walkway.

The stack of books she had been carrying scattered around them. Jay lay on his stomach, a college textbook on biochemistry open beneath his nose, the pages fluttering against his cheek in the crisp winter wind. He levered himself up to a sitting position and, with a grunt of frustration, pushed away from the wriggling body trapped beneath his legs.

The woman, dressed in a shapeless gray wool coat, rolled over. Snow caked her face and glasses. An unattractive knit hat hung lopsidedly from her head, hiding her hair. She pulled herself to her knees and scrambled blindly through the snow to find her notebook.

"Phenylethylamine," she muttered. "But then what? Damn!"

Irked by her casual disregard, Jay reached out to brush the snow away from her glasses, but she slapped at his hand and completed the task herself, revealing an angry glare.

"You see there?" she picked up the snow-covered notebook and held it out to him. "Now I've forgotten. A brilliant revelation gone, and all because of you!" She pulled off her glasses and wiped the smeared lenses with her damp mittens, then gave up and put them back on. "I may never get it back. I assume you have an explanation for this . . . this unprovoked attack?"

Jay pushed to his feet, then impatiently held out a hand to her. She pointedly ignored him and struggled to stand without help. She was small compared with his six-foot-one-inch height, maybe five-foot-three or four at the most. But in her angry state she appeared taller, her steely-spined posture nearly eclipsing his frame. He let his eyes wander over her figure. Beneath the dowdy coat and practical snowboots was a female body of indeterminate shape and age. He brought his gaze back to her painfully plain face, devoid of makeup and made plainer still by wire-rimmed glasses that were slightly askew. A strand of dark hair brushed against her cheek in the wind and she reached up and tucked it back beneath the ridiculous hat, hiding the only evidence of her femininity.

"Well?" she prompted.

"Well, what?" Jay returned.

"Now that you're through examining me, I'm waiting for your explanation. If it is credible, you may apologize and we can both be on our way. If not, I'm afraid I'll be forced to report this incident to the campus police."

"You want me to apologize?"

"In the social context of this situation, that would be the appropriate action."

"You want *me* to apologize," he repeated with a laugh.

"I believe I've made that very clear. You've knocked me into a snowbank, causing me to lose a very important train of thought. My notes are ruined. I think it's the least you could do."

"Listen, lady. At the very *least*, I should toss you right back into that snowbank. You step out in front of my car, I swerve to avoid hitting you and hit the curb, instead, ruining the alignment on my car, and you expect *me* to apologize to you. All you've got out of this whole episode is a soggy notebook. I'm left with a five-hundred-dollar car repair."

She looked at him vacantly. "What are you talking about?"

With a snort of disgust, Jay grabbed her arm and led her toward his car. "My car. You stepped off the curb in front of me and I had to swerve to avoid you."

"That's ridiculous."

"I agree. And it's also true. I think you're the one who owes me an apology."

She leaned down to look at the front tires of the car. "There doesn't appear to be any damage," she said calmly.

"Lady, I could have killed you!"

She looked up at him with wide brown eyes. "But you didn't," she replied in a matter-of-fact tone.

"But I could have. Or seriously injured you. You should never ever cross the street without looking both ways."

Now it was her turn to examine him. He watched her gaze run from his face to his toes and back again. She shook her head.

"I doubt that you would have hit me. You are a man of reasonable fitness and quick reflexes. Visibility was good and your vision unimpaired. Though the braking performance of your car may have been a variable, you seem to take great pride in this automobile. The brakes are most likely in good condition. Therefore, I forgive you for nearly running me down."

He grabbed her by the shoulders and gave her a shake. "You must be in shock," he said, searching her face for some clue to her condition.

"I assure you, I'm not in shock."

"But I could have killed you."

"But you didn't."

"Why do you keep saying that? Like everything is either black or white, right or wrong, on or off. Aren't you the least bit concerned that you could have been seriously injured?"

"The fact is, I am perfectly fine. There is no reason to be concerned over what could have been. What is *is*, and what could have been is of no consequence."

"Wait, let me guess," he said snidely. "Philosophy 101."

"Graduate-level common sense." She pushed her coat sleeve up and looked at her watch. "I'm late. I have to go." She turned from him and walked back to the snowbank to retrieve her books. He followed at her heels.

"What about my car?" he demanded as he stood over her.

"I don't see how I'm responsible for damage done to your car. When you chose to run into the curb, that was entirely beyond my control." She hefted the stack of books into the crook of her arm, straightened and began to walk away.

"Wait just a minute, sweetheart. Come back here. You and I aren't through discussing this!"

She turned back to him with an annoyed sigh. "There is one other variable in this equation. The speed limit on campus is ten miles per hour. If you had been observing the proper speed limit, I'm ninety-nine percent certain that you would have been able to stop your vehicle without having to swerve into the curb. Now, I really am running late. Have a nice day."

Speechless with rage, Jay watched her walk down the street. "Have a nice day?" he muttered. "Have a nice day?" he yelled to her retreating form. "You have a real nice day, too, sister. Maybe next time, if you're lucky, you'll step in front of a bus. And if *I'm* lucky, he won't miss!"

Women! He hated when they were right. And they did have an annoying habit of being right more often than not lately. So maybe he had been traveling faster than the speed limit. She certainly didn't need to be so smug and self-righteous about it.

He had come to Wisconsin to escape his problems with women and, once again, his life had been upset by one. Baltimore had become unlivable thanks to the female sex. All right, maybe he had made a mistake dating three women at once, but everything had been running so smoothly. He had the cool and confident Kristina for those formal business functions and symphony concerts. Then there was Shelly, athletic and outdoorsy, for those Saturday sails on the Chesapeake and long hikes through the woods surrounding his home. And finally there was Emily, an incredible cook with a wicked sense of humor.

He had thought he had everything under control, but then—*kaboom!*—the whole arrangement had blown up in his face. Emily found out about Kristina and then Kristina found out about Shelly. Then somehow they all got together to trade stories. Before he knew it, his life had become a living hell.

When he'd been offered the opportunity to spend a semester as a guest lecturer at Wisconsin State University in Riversbend he had jumped at the chance to get out of Baltimore. Beaumont Boatyards could practically run itself, thanks to the competent general manager he had hired a year ago. And the other divisions of Beaumont Industries were also in good hands. A respite from work and women would give him the quiet time to concentrate on his pet project, a book on the history of naval engineering.

And Riversbend also had Mitch Kincaid. The fact that his Naval Academy roommate was on the faculty was the deciding vote. Jay hadn't seen Mitch in nearly seven years, not since Mitch had left the navy to pursue an academic life and Jay had taken over the family boat-building business.

So Jay began a self-imposed Wisconsin vacation and spent his evenings playing racquetball and basketball with his old buddy. During the day, he lectured in undergraduate marketing courses, taught graduate-level business seminars and worked on *The Early History of U.S. Naval Engineering*.

It hadn't been hard to avoid women at Wisconsin State. Giggling coeds bored him and aggressive female professors left him cold. The only attractive women left in Riversbend were married and the only single women were either on the near side of eighteen or the far side of sixty-five. In a town that rolled up its streets at dusk, the type of sophisticated single women Jay was used to dating had fled long ago. Either that or they all hibernated for the winter.

But wasn't this monkish life-style exactly what he wanted?

Jay shook his head disgustedly, then climbed into his car and backed away from the curb. He was already fifteen minutes late for his graduate seminar on interna-

tional marketing. His overly-enthusiastic students would
no doubt be waiting patiently for him. Now was no time
to ponder his lack of a social life.

As he drove down the street to the other end of the
campus, he kept a watchful eye on the curb. That woman
was a bona fide menace to the driving public. There was
no telling where she might strike next.

"WHAT HAPPENED to you?"

Dr. Susannah Hart shrugged out of her damp coat and
pulled her snow-caked hat from her head. Her glasses
had fogged the minute she'd walked into Science Hall and
she was having trouble seeing her graduate assistant,
Lauren McMahon, through the lenses. Susannah wasn't
quite sure how to answer Lauren's question without
sounding completely ridiculous. And Susannah Hart
made it a point never to sound ridiculous.

"Nothing important. I fell . . . into a snowbank." She
pulled off her glasses, letting them dangle around her
neck from their chain, then kicked off her boots and
quickly walked to the opposite wall of her lab to peer into
a small cage. "I'm sorry I'm late. How's Max?" she asked.
"Any change?"

Lauren walked over and stuck her finger through the
cage. A large white rat waddled through the shredded
newspaper and sniffed at her fingertip. "Max is in love,"
Lauren answered in an excited voice.

Susannah turned to her in disbelief. "Are you sure?"

Lauren nodded and smiled. "As sure as I can be. If you
don't believe me, ask Minnie." She pointed to the ad-
joining cage, where a smaller rat lay curled in the corner, sound asleep. "Poor Minnie doesn't know what hit
her. It was definitely love at first sight."

"Where's the data?" Susannah asked.

Lauren handed her a folder and Susannah scanned the lab report. "You made sure to cross-check all the tests?"

"I checked and double-checked and cross-checked three times."

"Formulation number nine." Susannah finally allowed herself a small, satisfied smile. "Do you know what this means?"

Lauren nodded. "It means that the brilliant Dr. Susannah Hart, with the help of her capable lab assistant, Lauren McMahon, has developed the world's first love potion."

"The first love potion for rats," Susannah amended. "And both you and I know, rats rarely need help with sexual attraction. We still don't know if the potion will work on humans."

"It will," Lauren assured her excitedly. "I just know it will."

Susannah slid onto a lab stool. After three years of work—long days and endless nights, failed potions and dead-end research—she finally had a breakthrough. When she began her research on the chemistry of love she had no idea where it would lead. It hadn't even been her primary research focus, merely an offshoot of her main research on the mating habits of the North American mud turtle. But then she stumbled upon the research of behavioral scientist Dr. Louisa Gruber. Before long, Susannah's time and interest were completely occupied by her potion research. She was determined to prove that if love was truly based in chemistry, as Dr. Gruber had claimed, it could be controlled like any other chemical reaction. She would prove that love was not the all-consuming fairy-tale emotion that the world made it out to be.

The applications of the potion were mind-boggling. Dr. Louise Gruber's landmark research had proven that sexual attraction, infatuation and love were caused by the brain's chemical reaction to another human being. Life experiences, genetic imprinting and sense of smell all combined to pair off men and women in a never-ending procession to the altar. Unfortunately the body developed an immunity to the initial rush of lust around the fourth year, initiating another never-ending procession—through the divorce courts. Couples who survived what current theory dubbed the "four-year itch" usually avoided divorce and found happiness in a lifetime commitment. Children seemed to delay the onset, but sadly, one out of every two couples in the United States succumbed to the "itch" sooner or later.

If Susannah succeeded, her potion could change that dismal scenario. She had bypassed Dr. Gruber's research on life experiences and genetic imprinting and concentrated her studies on the effect of smell on sexual attraction. Her potion, worn like perfume, would be specifically designed for the target subject's genetic makeup. Although scentless, the pheromone would set off the chemical reaction in the brain that produced sexual attraction, making the subject irresistibly drawn to the wearer.

"So what's the next step, Susannah?"

Susannah cupped her chin in her hand and continued to watch Max as the chubby rat poked his nose through the cage. She reached for a bag of peanut-butter cookies on the counter. "I know you'd probably prefer a cigarette, Max," Susannah whispered, "but cookies are much better for your health." She shoved a piece of cookie into the cage, then faced Lauren.

"We need to run a series of controlled field tests on human subjects. The potion works on our lab rats, but before I open my research up to my colleagues, I want to be sure we're not wandering down the wrong road."

"But once we start looking for research subjects, won't the word get out?" Lauren asked. "If Dr. Curtis finds out about our work, he'll blow a major artery. Love potion experiments aren't on Fred Curtis's list of acceptable and politically correct research. He's already got his graduate assistant spying on us. The little weasel has been in here twice this morning looking for you."

"Dr. Curtis will gladly support this research once he realizes the potential publicity it will bring the university. And don't worry, I can handle Derwin."

"Good morning, Dr. Hart . . . Ms. McMahon."

Susannah and Lauren slowly turned to find the weasel in question standing in the doorway of the lab. Derwin Erwin, graduate assistant to department chairman Dr. Frederick Curtis, resembled the mammal in more ways than one. Gangly legs and arms and a stick-thin body made him appear as though he had never quite made it out of puberty. He wore his scraggly hair combed straight back and held in place with what Susannah guessed was some type of hair tonic. To top it all off, he seemed to suffer from a permanent case of the sniffles. She watched as his eyes darted around the lab, no doubt looking for some tidbit of impropriety he could report back to his boss.

Susannah's lab assistant had often used Derwin as a yardstick for measuring sexual appeal. Derwin, with his whiny voice, his high-water pants and his heavy metal T-shirts, hovered near the bottom of Lauren's yardstick. At the top was some man named Mel Gibson, probably one of Lauren's numerous boyfriends, Susannah had deduced.

Susannah trusted Lauren's opinion on the matter. After all, Lauren knew much more about sexy men than Susannah. But when she remembered the guy in the Jaguar, Susannah knew he would definitely be near the top—on anyone's scale.

"Hello, Erwin," Lauren muttered. "Who let you out of your cage?"

"Hardy-har-har," Derwin replied. "You're so funny I forgot to laugh."

"You also forgot your personality today, didn't you, Derwin?" Lauren continued. "Hey, if I come across it, I'll be sure to return it. Though I may need an electron microscope to find it."

Derwin held up a clipboard and stared at it in a pretentious fashion. "Dr. Curtis is looking for last week's research update, Dr. Hart," he said in his nasal whine. "According to my records, you haven't turned it in. I'm sure you're aware that Dr. Curtis has the power to withhold your funding. I would suggest you have the report on his desk no later than tomorrow morning."

"I filed that report, Mr. Erwin," Susannah said. "I put it on your desk last Friday as you requested."

"You did? Hmm." Derwin casually walked over to the counter and bent down to look at Max and Minnie. "That's strange," Derwin said.

"Maybe if you'd clean off your desk, you'd find what you're looking for," Lauren answered.

"I didn't mean the lost report, Ms. McMahon. As I understand it, your research grant has to do with the North American mud turtle. Reptilia from the order Chelonia, genus *Kinosternon*."

"My lab assistant knows her taxonomic classifications, Mr. Erwin," Susannah replied warily. "And, as always, we are impressed with your own vast knowledge. What is your point?"

"All I ever see in this lab is *Rattus*, class Mammalia, order Rodentia. Warm-blooded mammals." Derwin scribbled something on his clipboard. "My point, Dr. Hart, is that mud turtles are cold-blooded reptiles. How could your research possibly involve warm-blooded lab animals?"

Susannah stood and gently took Derwin by the arm, guiding him to the door. "The world is filled with many strange and mysterious creatures, Mr. Erwin. You've proved that fact time and time again...in your own very important research, I mean." She led him into the hallway, then stepped back inside the lab and grabbed the edge of the door. "So why don't you get back to it?" she added as she quietly shut the door in his face.

Susannah turned and leaned back against the door with a sigh. "Has Derwin been nosier than usual lately or is it just my own paranoia?"

"He's been nosier. Do you think he knows what we're working on?"

Susannah shook her head. "No, at least not yet. But to be on the safe side, we'd better bring in some mud turtles to satisfy his curiosity. And I'll take Max and Minnie home with me. I just wish there were some way to stop Derwin's meddling for good," Susannah said.

"You and me both," Lauren replied. "The little *Twerpus stupidus* really gets on my nerves. He and Curtis take credit for every important breakthrough in this department, whether they've had anything to do with it or not. I just like to rattle his cage every now and then. Besides, why should I pretend to like him?"

"You don't have to like him, but it might be wise if you refrained from goading him," Susannah suggested. "Why don't you try to be nicer to him? As my mother used to tell me, you can catch more men with honey than you can with vinegar."

"I thought that was flies. Or bees."

"Not with my mother." Susannah smiled ruefully and sighed. "And speaking of catching men, let's get back to work. On the subject of research subjects, we will first need to define our parameters. I would suggest we concentrate on an initial field test using just one subject, then gradually expand our base after we work the wrinkles out. All our work has centered on the potion being worn by a female, so our initial target subject must be a male. A male with a strong aversion to love and commitment."

"A confirmed bachelor?" Lauren asked.

"Yes, exactly."

"Well, there's no shortage of those in the world these days. I can vouch for that."

"We need a man who has no predilection toward our female subject. Yet a man who has shown a marked preference for beautiful, outgoing women...*many* beautiful, outgoing women. We need to find someone here in Riversbend, someone we can keep a close watch on. And don't forget we have to have a sample for the DNA testing." Susannah frowned. "A hair follicle would be the best, but even that could be a problem. How are we going to get a strand of his hair without him—"

"Wait!" Lauren cried. "I have the perfect candidate." She hurried over to her desk, tucked away in a corner of the lab, and began rummaging through a tall pile of papers that threatened to topple at any moment. "Here it is," she said triumphantly, waving a copy of the uni-

versity's faculty newsletter. "And here *he* is." She placed
the open newsletter in front of Susannah and pointed to
a photograph.

Susannah looked closely at the photo, fumbling for
her glasses. As she slid them on, the image came into
sharper focus and Susannah's breath caught in her
throat. She immediately recognized the man, even
though when she had encountered him, less than an hour
ago, his handsome face had been tensed in anger.

"Isn't he gorgeous?" Lauren said. "His name is Jay
Beaumont and he's here for a semester as a guest lecturer
in the School of Business. He owns a successful company in Baltimore, something to do with boats or ships.
My roommate Lisa works over at Creighton Hall and
says all the women over there are madly in love with him.
Rumor has it that he's a real playboy and, to quote Lisa,
'a confirmed bachelor.' Yet he's been avoiding women on
this campus like the plague."

Susannah continued to stare at the photograph, her
mind spinning with the possibilities. The idea was absurd. Still, it could work. And what better way to field
test her potion and maintain secrecy on her work? And
there was no denying that the man would make a perfect
target subject. He fit all the requirements.

Susannah drew a deep breath, then released it very
slowly. "He's perfect," she said. She drew her finger along
the outline of his strong jaw, then moved it across his firm
mouth. He was an incredible specimen, handsome,
compelling, his chiseled features in flawless balance—
straight nose, high cheekbones, striking eyes. Undeni-
ably masculine. "Absolutely perfect, in fact."

"Great," Lauren replied. "And let me be the first to
volunteer my services as the female half of this experiment."

"Actually, I have someone else in mind. A woman who would keep our experiment in the strictest of confidence. Someone Mr. Beaumont has preexisting negative feelings for. A rather plain woman with unremarkable physical assets. Just the type Mr. Beaumont would show no natural attraction to."

Lauren eyed her suspiciously. "Who do you have in mind, Susannah?"

"Me," Susannah stated.

"You?" Lauren's eyes went wide with shock.

Susannah nodded decisively. "I'm the perfect candidate for the experiment. Jay Beaumont already hates me. We met this morning. He claims I caused his car to smash into a curb. I believe his precise parting sentiment was that he hoped I'd be hit by a bus. And I am certainly not his type. I'm not a beauty and I'm somewhat introverted when it comes to men. I'm too short and I don't have an attractive figure. I'm also a bit older than the women he probably dates. I'm the ideal choice."

Lauren frowned and shook her head. "Susannah, why do you always run yourself down? With a tiny bit of work, you could be a very attractive woman. Take your hair, for instance. You hide it in that prim little bun all the time, all pulled back from your face." Lauren got up and pushed Susannah down onto her stool. Standing behind her, she carefully removed the hairpins and combs from Susannah's hair, then spread the thick mass across her back and over her shoulders.

Susannah looked over her shoulder. "You see. It's not attractive at all. My hair is too frizzy and kinky and it's an ugly brown color." How many times had she heard those same words from her mother? *Why couldn't you have inherited my lovely pale hair,* her mother had complained, *instead of your father's mop?*

"I would kill for hair like this," Lauren replied. "Women spend hours at the hair stylist to get their hair to curl like yours. It's not frizzy—it's wavy. And your hair isn't just plain brown—it's mahogany."

"It's not blond. Or straight and smooth like yours."

"No, it's not, but it's gorgeous just the same. Now, take your glasses off and come over here."

Susannah slowly pulled her glasses off and followed Lauren to a huge, glass-doored lab cabinet in which she could see her reflection.

Lauren fluffed and pulled at Susannah's hair, then ordered her to unbutton the top two buttons of her conservative white blouse. Over Susannah's objections, she snatched away the plain tie that was knotted in a neat bow around her neck and wove it through Susannah's hair. Then Lauren forced her to remove the gray wool blazer she wore and replaced it with her own brightly colored tapestry vest. Finally, she pulled mascara, lipstick and blusher from her purse and artfully applied them to Susannah's grimacing face.

When she was finished, Susannah found herself staring at a stranger. A young and vibrant woman who looked much more attractive than the plain Dr. Susannah Hart. A woman who appeared almost . . . sexy.

"See," Lauren murmured. "I told you. If I wasn't your friend, I'd never recognize you."

"Friend?" Susannah asked softly, surprised by Lauren's declaration. She gazed at her reflection. She had never had a real girlfriend. Even as a child she had preferred solitude to the social maneuverings that finding a friend required. Instead she'd stayed on the sidelines, a detached observer, a junior research scientist, evaluating, comparing, concluding. Besides, her single-minded devotion to study had only served to drive her classmates farther away with taunts of "brown nose" and "teacher's pet," "egghead" and "bookworm."

When her mother had lobbied to send her to a private girl's school, hoping that in the proper environment her shy, fourteen-year-old daughter would bloom, Susannah had rejoiced. Her mother's attention had recently been diverted by her new husband, an arrogant and impatient art dealer. And Susannah spent little time with her father, who only intimidated her with his distant manner. Boarding school sounded like heaven, with twenty-four-hour-a-day access to academics and the possibility of finding a friend who shared her love for books.

At first her father had refused to pay the exorbitant tuition and board for the exclusive school and Susannah had become a pawn in another power struggle. But as her freshman year in public high school progressed, she became more and more withdrawn. Finally her father relented, and she was placed at the Emily Dickinson Academy for Young Ladies, where her academics flourished. Unfortunately her social skills remained dormant. She was a wallflower that stubbornly refused to bloom.

Susannah sighed, then shot Lauren a wavering smile. "This is all very nice, Lauren. But it's really not me. I feel silly, uncomfortable . . ." Her hand fluttered at her open collar. "Exposed."

"Don't sell yourself short," Lauren said as she pushed her hands away. "You look beautiful and alluring. You have to stop hiding behind those dorky glasses and that old-maid hairdo."

Susannah smiled at Lauren's blunt assessment. Since the day Lauren had been assigned to her lab two years ago, Susannah had felt a connection to her. With only five years difference in their ages, Lauren had blithely ignored Susannah's reticence and treated her as if they were fast friends. They gossiped and laughed, they shared their most intimate and embarrassing stories and they spoke of their dreams and aspirations. Lauren had become both a best friend and a surrogate sister to Susannah, but Susannah was afraid to admit it out loud, afraid that Lauren would discover the real Susannah Hart and find her as uninteresting as the girls at Emily Dickinson had.

"But my plain looks are an important component of the experiment," Susannah replied.

Lauren smiled knowingly. "Not to the first phase of our experiment."

"The first phase. What first phase?"

"Have you forgotten the hair sample? We can't formulate an effective potion unless we find a way to test Jay Beaumont's DNA."

Susannah sighed. "And how do you propose we get a sample of Jay Beaumont's hair?"

Lauren smiled slyly. "I have a plan."

"I DON'T THINK this is a very good plan," Susannah said, her voice filled with doubt. She stood in front of a full-length mirror in the corner of Lauren McMahon's bedroom.

"What better way to get a piece of Jay Beaumont's hair?" Lauren replied.

"But what if someone recognizes me?"

"Susannah, look at yourself. Can you honestly believe the woman you see in that mirror is Dr. Susannah Hart?"

Susannah let her gaze wander down her reflected image. Her hair was freshly washed and styled and it looked . . . well, it looked big. Her wide eyes were ringed by soft dark eyeliner and mascara-touched lashes. Her glasses were gone, replaced by green contact lenses she had never bothered to wear. And her cheeks and lips were rouged subtly.

"Brightly colored plumage," she mumbled to herself.

"What?" Lauren asked, looking up from the floor, where she worked on shortening the hem of a terribly skimpy red sequined dress.

"One of the important criteria for choosing a mate in the Aves classification is the presence of beautiful plumage. A female bird will search for the most brilliantly colored male to mate with. It is a sign of status. Somehow the process got switched around for humans, though. It is the female in the human race who sports the most brilliant plumage."

"Well, you're not going to get much more brilliant than this, Dr. Hart."

Susannah stared at the glittering dress that molded itself to every curve of her body. "I don't know, Lauren. Don't you think this dress is a little too . . . revealing?"

"That's the point. You have to display your assets."

Susannah turned and looked over her shoulder into the mirror at the plunging back and the thigh-high hem. "If I bend over, I'm liable to display more than just my assets." She turned back around. "In the animal kingdom, the male seeks a female who is sturdy and capable of bearing the young, a female who can protect the lair and forage for food."

She peeked down the front of the dress, noting the extra fabric left unfilled. At least the wide collar served one purpose: it hid her rather unremarkable chest. Lauren's figure was much more . . . developed than hers. "Men like tall, athletic women with substantial breasts and hips."

"Don't worry about your breasts and hips," Lauren
assured her. "You have plenty to fill out this dress. In fact,
you've got a lovely figure. I don't know why you insist
on hiding it beneath those unflattering clothes."

Susannah smoothed the dress over her hips, looking
at her figure objectively. Maybe Lauren was right. She
didn't look too repulsive in the dress. "But I'm not tall,"
she stated. "Genetic imprinting will cause the male human to gravitate toward a female who is tall. Whether
men realize it or not, they are simply following the instincts of their caveman ancestors."

"Yes, but unlike our cavewoman ancestors, we have
these."

Susannah looked down at Lauren, who held up a pair
of red high-heeled shoes. Lauren slid them on Susannah's feet, elevating her another three inches.

"I've never considered that high heels are simply a
form of physical compensation," Susannah murmured.
"I always assumed they were merely some ridiculous
male invention, a throwback to medieval torture." She
took a tentative step, then another, admiring the way the
heels gave her figure more stature, a more powerful
presence. She had always worn flats, sensible shoes that
were comfortable to work in and walk in. Maybe she had
been missing an important means of asserting herself in
a male-dominated world. And big hair certainly didn't
hurt the cause, either.

"Actually, high heels were invented by the French
queen Catherine de Médicis in the sixteenth century,"
Lauren replied. "I discovered that fact while I was doing
research for you on human sexual response. And I really
doubt that she had genetic imprinting in mind. Heels alter a woman's posture, arching the back, thrusting the
breasts and buttocks out and elongating the line of the

ankle." Lauren grinned. "But then again, maybe old Catherine knew more about male sexual response than we give her credit for."

Lauren rose to stand beside Susannah. "Well, I'm finished with my part. Dr. Susannah Hart is dressed to kill."

Susannah crinkled her nose and forced a smile. "I don't think I can go through with this. I'm a scientist, not a . . . a . . . hussy."

"Susannah, the plan is very simple. You show up at the faculty reception for Jay Beaumont. You catch his eye, flirt a little, run your fingers through his hair and presto! You've got what you came for. Here, take this hair spray along. Spritz a little on your fingers to make them sticky."

"But I've never flirted before in my life."

"You're an expert in human sexual response. Take the word of someone who's done research for you. You know every advance and response in the book and now's the time to apply what you know."

"But what if someone recognizes me?" she asked again.

"Trust me," Lauren said with a sigh. "No one will recognize you."

"Why can't *you* do this?" Susannah pleaded.

"Because someone is sure to recognize me," Lauren explained. "I go to these receptions all the time. It's a great way to meet men. But you haven't attended a faculty reception since the one they gave in your honor when you came to Wisconsin State five years ago."

"You know how I hate those receptions. All that small talk and political maneuvering. At least come with me. If I need some help, we can rendezvous in the ladies' room."

After a long moment, Lauren finally nodded her agreement. "All right, I'll come along. But only to lend discreet moral support." She grabbed her purse and coat from the bed.

"Aren't you going to change?" Susannah asked.

Lauren laughed. "No one is going to give me a second glance with you in the room, Susannah."

Her offhand compliment gave Susannah a small boost of badly needed courage. She pulled on the elegant beaded jacket that Lauren had lent her for the evening and picked up a black handbag. Then she took a deep breath and let it out very slowly. "All right, I'm ready."

Lauren hesitated, her brow furrowed. "No, you're not."

"I'm not?"

"We forgot about your name. How are you going to introduce yourself? We need a sexy name."

Susannah turned back to look at herself in the mirror. A nervous smile twitched at the corners of her mouth. Slowly she pushed her bottom lip out in a well-calculated pout, a technique Dr. Gruber had described in great detail in her last book. Her eyelids lowered slightly as her mouth curved up in a suggestive smile. Then she reached up and ran her fingers through her hair, shaking her head. "Desirée," she said in low, husky voice. "My name is Desirée Smith."

With that, Susannah turned from the mirror and wobbled through Lauren's apartment to the front door, all the way feeling every bit like another famous French queen. Marie-Antoinette . . . on her way to the guillotine.

2

JAY HAD ALREADY decided to leave and was on his way to
the door when she arrived. Her glittering dress stopped
him faster than a flashing red light at a busy intersec-
tion. Beside him, Mitch drew a sharp breath, then exhaled slowly, mirroring Jay's own reaction to the woman.
She stood in the doorway, surveying the crowd, her gaze
flitting from one face to another, never alighting for more
than an instant. One by one, the men in the room turned
to stare, suspending their conversations until the noisy
cocktail chatter had diminished by half.

She blinked slowly, the only acknowledgment of the
stir she was causing, and ran the tip of her tongue along
her top and then her bottom lip, an action that first appeared self-conscious, but was no doubt calculatingly
sensual. Jay knew the signals. She couldn't have made
her intentions any clearer if she'd had SEDUCE ME
written across her forehead. The woman was definitely
looking for a good time.

Her gaze met his and there she lingered for one long,
suggestive moment. Then her eyelids dropped coyly.
When she looked back up, her gaze had shifted to Mitch,
and Jay saw her eyes widen slightly in recognition before
moving away.

"Who is she?" Jay asked.

"I don't know," Mitch replied. "I've never seen her before in my life."

"Are you sure? She seemed to recognize you."

Mitch dragged his gaze from the woman, who was now weaving her way to the bar, and frowned at Jay. "Unlike you, Beaumont, I remember every woman I've ever dated. I remember every woman I've ever slept with, by name. And I also remember every woman I've ever met who looks like that one. I've never met, dated or slept with her. Believe me, I'd remember."

Jay clapped his friend on the shoulder. "Good, then you won't mind if I introduce myself."

"I thought you'd sworn off women," Mitch grumbled. "Didn't you just tell me that less than ten minutes ago?"

He had made that resolution. After this morning's near accident, he had become even more convinced that he should stay as far away from women as possible. It had been easy up until now. But Jay had been cloistered for entirely too long in this sleepy Wisconsin town. Now there was a good reason to break his vow of chastity, and she had wild mahogany hair and a sexy mouth and a curvy little figure made just for his hands. "I may have said that," Jay admitted. "In a brief moment of insanity. But only after you suggested that blind date with Dr. What's-her-name."

"Susannah Hart is her name. And she's a brilliant biochemist and a very nice lady. We met when we planned an oceanography symposium a couple of years ago. She's a little shy, but she's got a great sense of humor. And I didn't suggest a date—I suggested dinner."

"If she's so great, why don't *you* date her?" Jay asked, punctuating his question with a poke of his beer bottle.

Mitch gave him a derisive look. "She's a friend. And this wouldn't be a date."

"A date that wouldn't be a date. Great concept, but I know exactly where this is leading. Why does everyone on this planet, you and my mother included, feel compelled to alter my marital status? I'm thirty-five years old. I've got at least another ten or twenty years of fun left in me."

"Wait a second," Mitch protested. "Who said anything about marriage?"

"Can you honestly say that the phrase 'She'd make some man a wonderful wife' never entered your mind?"

"And what's wrong with that? There's more to a woman than a gorgeous face and a great body. You've been searching for the perfect woman for years—ever since Cynthia. Haven't you learned anything yet?"

Jay controlled his expression at the mention of his ex-wife's name. "Sure. I've learned there's no such thing as the perfect woman. Cynthia proved that. And without the perfect woman, there can be no perfect relationship and thereby no perfect marriage. So, I've resigned myself to terminal bachelorhood."

Even as he spoke the words, Jay knew he really didn't mean them. He wanted a "happily ever after." He wanted a wife and children, but he wasn't willing to put his heart on the line. He had done that once and once was enough. The breakup of his marriage had left him stunned, numb with anger and distrust. He had loved Cynthia to distraction, carefully constructing his life and his future around her and the children they would have. One day, the marriage had all seemed perfect, and the next day, she was gone. She had packed her bags and left him for another man, a man he had once considered his best friend, a man he had known his entire life. She had been living a lie since their wedding day, she had explained in the note. And so had he, only he hadn't known it.

For two years, he'd mourned his stupidity and naïveté. But then he'd begun dating again, and with each new conquest, he'd buried the pain deeper within him. Women were a soothing balm, an antidote to the loneliness that lay in wait. He had locked his ability to love tightly away, in a Pandora's box, never to be opened again. And there it had remained, for ten years.

"If I'm forced to put up with imperfections," Jay muttered, "then she might as well be nice to look at."

"Maybe you're looking in the wrong place."

He scowled. "Why are you so determined to fix us up? I sense an ulterior motive here. Come on, Kincaid. Level with me and maybe I'll consider it."

Mitch shrugged as he took a long swallow of his beer, then explained. "Susannah has a lab assistant, Lauren McMahon. I've seen her a few times at Susannah's office, but we can't get past the small-talk stage. I thought we could all have dinner together—you know, break the ice."

"Bad choice of words, Kincaid. Any woman you have to compare to ice isn't worth the time and effort. I prefer my women hot, not frozen solid. And that lady in the red dress is definitely at optimum temperature."

"Lauren is worth it. She's incredibly smart and she's—" Mitch stopped suddenly.

"She's what?" Jay turned to see Mitch's jaw drop open. "She's got a great sense of humor, right?"

"She's here," Mitch said in a strangled whisper. "Over there, near the bar. Wait, don't look . . . okay, now look. But don't look like you're looking. She's the tall blonde with the flowered vest."

Jay whistled softly. "Very nice. For a minute there, Kincaid, I was actually starting to worry about you."

"You can stop worrying. And you can quit looking now. She is strictly off-limits."

"Okay by me. So why don't you just take out your ice pick and talk to your friend Lauren while I go get my socks melted by the honey in the red dress."

Mitch shook his head. "Your arrogance amazes me, Beaumont. Just when did you corner the market on charisma?"

"It's taken years and years of dedicated practice, Mitch, my boy." Jay tipped his bottle of beer to Mitch, then drained it. He zeroed in on his target and shoved the empty bottle at his friend. "If you're really interested, I'll explain it all to you—tomorrow morning."

"I TOLD YOU this wouldn't work!" Susannah whispered through a tight smile. "He's talking to Mitch. How am I supposed to get close to him now? What if Mitch recognizes me?"

Lauren turned away from the bar and faced the room. "Give it time. He's just playing it cool. Sooner or later he's bound to leave Mitch and move in for a closer look. After that scorching eye contact you made, he'd be a fool not to."

"It's called the 'copulatory gaze.' Dr. Gruber says it's a courting cue. It's been studied very closely in baboons," Susannah explained. "I hold his gaze for three or four seconds, then lower my eyelids and glance away. It's supposed to indicate my interest. I did it just like the book said, but it didn't work. According to Dr. Gruber, he's supposed to make the next move. Four other men have responded and I wasn't even gazing at them! Why hasn't he?" Susannah pulled open her purse and took out a small notepad. "I must be doing something wrong."

"Be patient," Lauren replied. "It doesn't always work the—what's that?"

"My notes." She frantically flipped through the pages, reviewing Dr. Gruber's five steps in the courting process. "Awareness, acknowledgment, verbalization, body contact, synchrony," she murmured. She repeated them again to herself, then shoved the notepad back in her purse.

"Susannah, you know this stuff cold. Just relax and— Oh-oh. Shark at ten o'clock."

Susannah yanked her notes out of her purse again. "What? Is it him?"

"Put that away!" Lauren warned. "I gotta go. Good luck."

Susannah felt a presence beside her at the bar. She shoved the notepad down the front of her dress, then grabbed her wineglass and took a gulp of warm Chablis. Slowly she turned, a smile pasted on her face. But the smile faded as she looked up at the pompous expression of her department chairman, Dr. Frederick Curtis.

She should have known he'd be here! Dr. Curtis was a confirmed philanderer and never missed an opportunity to practice his lechery. He fancied himself as academia's answer to Casanova. A handsome, though patently vain man in his midfifties, he usually left his wife at home during faculty parties, preferring to turn his attention to attractive women professors and fawning graduate students. He had never made a move on her. Until now.

"Hello, there," he said smoothly. "Can I buy you a drink?"

Susannah turned back to the bar and tugged her hair across her cheek to hide her face. Then she remembered that toying with one's hair was a major component of the "awareness" stage. What if he recognized her? Besides Lauren, there were only a few people who knew her well

enough to recognize Desirée Smith as Susannah Hart.
Mitch Kincaid was one. And the other was eyeing her
bosom with ill-disguised intent.

"Ah... no, thank you. I—my glass is still..." She
peered into her nearly empty glass and stifled a groan.

*Get control of yourself, Susannah. You're a profes-
sional, well versed in the dynamics of human sexuality,
not some babbling bimbo. And this is research.*

"No. Thanks, anyway. I've had enough."

"But you just got here," he replied. "The party's just
started." He moved closer and the smell of his cologne
made her stomach churn. "What's your name?"

Susannah straightened and faced him. She forced a
smile. "My name?"

"I haven't seen you at these receptions before. Are you
new on campus?"

"Yes... yes, I'm new." His cold, clammy finger
skimmed up her forearm and her skin crawled with distaste. *Oh, dear, body contact! Stage four!*

"Well, let me be the first to welcome you to Wisconsin
State. I'm Frederick Curtis. *Dr.* Frederick Curtis. I'm
chairman of the Biology Department." He paused. "And
you're?"

He hadn't recognized her! It was as if he were looking
right past her at a total stranger. "Desirée," she ven-
tured. "Desirée Smith."

His finger moved to her upper arm and she shivered
in revulsion. She felt cornered, trapped, forced to play
out a normal flirtation. If only she could extract herself
from this situation without arousing his suspicion. She
stifled the urge to bolt for the door and put Lauren's ridiculous plan behind her.

No, she couldn't run. She had come here for a purpose and she wasn't going to leave until she had a strand

of Jay Beaumont's hair tucked safely in her purse. Burying her nervousness, she let her analytical mind take over. Though Dr. Curtis was predictably following the five steps in human courtship, he had managed to sprint through the first four in less than a minute. Susannah would have to put a stop to his runaway attention immediately.

"Tell me, Desirée, what's a girl with such a sexy name doing at a dull party like this?"

Susannah gave him a doe-eyed look, the same look she had seen him elicit from a number of female students in the Biology Department. "Did you say your name was Dr. Frederick Curtis?" Her voice was breathy, more from disgust than design.

He thrust out his chest. Susannah had studied the same inflative behavior in codfish and marveled at how her department head so closely resembled his counterpart in the piscine world.

"You've heard of me?"

With a sweet expression on her face, she ran her finger down the lapel of his tailored suit. "You aren't by any chance the husband of Carolyn Curtis, are you?" His eager look dissolved and he smiled nervously. She could almost feel the rush of air as his ego and his naughty intentions deflated.

"Why, yes, I am. Do you know Carolyn?"

"Oh, my, yes!" Susannah cried, looping her arm in his. "I met her at a recent luncheon and we became fast friends. I must call her and tell her that you and I have become—" she lowered her eyes winsomely "—acquainted. You will say hello to her for me, won't you?"

Curtis picked up his glass from the bar and nodded coldly as he pulled away from her. "Yes. Of course. Excuse me, I see Dr. Lewis over there. I must speak to him before I leave. It was nice meeting you, Des—Ms. Smith."

Susannah watched him hurry away, then searched the room for Lauren. She saw her lab assistant chatting pleasantly with Mitch Kincaid. At least he's out of the way, Susannah thought. She'd have to thank Lauren later for doing what was necessary to further the interests of science, including occupying Mitch Kincaid.

Susannah had met Mitch over a year ago and since then they had become close friends. A dedicated research scientist for the Great Lakes Institute and a respected colleague, Mitch understood the sacrifice involved in a life of science. They shared a satisfying professional friendship of weekly lunches and an occasional concert or lecture. Susannah counted only two people as friends—Lauren and Mitch. Lauren knew about her pheromone research, but Susannah had never discussed her secret work with Mitch. Though Mitch was Susannah's friend, she wasn't sure she could trust him with her secrets.

As Susannah watched Mitch and Lauren, the nature of their behavior began to sink in by degrees. Lauren's casual toss of her hair, her coy smile and intent gaze. Mitch's exaggerated body movements and preening behavior.

Lauren and Mitch were courting! And to Susannah's trained eye, Lauren was going so far as to act as if she were enjoying it. Susannah looked away, guilty for staring and for putting Lauren in such an uncomfortable position. But her professional curiosity drew her back to the pair. Odd, she thought. Lauren didn't seem uncomfortable in the least.

Her attention was diverted by a tall figure across the room and she suddenly remembered her reason for attending the reception. She watched as Jay Beaumont moved from one group of people to another. There it was. The swaggering movement, the utter male confidence that primatologists called bird-dogging. As he stood and conversed, she recognized the other signs of Dr. Gruber's "awareness" stage. He was establishing his territory and signaling his importance and she knew instinctively that she was the target of his behavior.

Susannah took a deep breath and began her foray into the courting ritual. She stretched slightly, arching her back, then turned and ordered another drink, shifting and swaying against the bar to the rhythm of the small jazz ensemble playing in the far corner. She covertly pulled her notebook out for a quick review, then pushed it back down the front of her dress. When she turned around again, he was staring at her. She returned his gaze and smiled. He smiled back. Phase two, she thought to herself as her pulse began to race. Acknowledgment.

Over the next ten minutes, they both moved around the room, advancing and retreating, her gaze locking with his for short, potent moments, then shifting away. She wandered to the buffet table and studied the selection. She was alone there and decided to await his approach and the next stage: conversation.

Susannah knew that the third stage was the most crucial, for the human voice revealed qualities that could either attract or repel a potential suitor. Intonation and inflection would give clues to her intentions. And her true intentions had to be subverted. Dr. Gruber claimed that a gentle, high-pitched, melodic voice was a sign of sexual interest. In her present state of nervousness, she wasn't sure her voice would work at all.

"Hello, my name is Desirée," she said softly to herself. If her voice was any higher, she'd risk shattering every champagne glass in the room.

"Hi, I'm Desirée," she repeated. Too low. She sounded as though she had just swallowed a bullfrog.

She took another shaky breath. "Hello—"

"Hello," a warm voice responded.

Susannah froze in front of the fruit platter. He was beside her, filling his own plate. He stood close—close enough for her to feel the heat radiating from his body. The smell of spicy soap and woodsy after-shave mingled in the air. She was tempted to take a deep breath and savor the clean, masculine smell, but was afraid she'd pass out or, at the least, hyperventilate. She moved along the table.

He followed her. "You might want to reconsider the cheese balls," he said benignly. "I understand Goodyear is using the recipe to develop a more durable tire."

A nervous giggle nearly burst from Susannah's throat at his sardonic wit, but she carefully curbed her response. As the studies had predicted, his comment fell into one of two probable subject areas. Food or her appearance. He had chosen food.

She glanced over at him, and suddenly her knees went weak and her pulse accelerated. She had thought him handsome when he'd railed at her over his car, but now he was even more magnificent.

"Really?" she murmured.

Really? What kind of response was that? As if she were gullible enough to believe his comment. She forced a flirtatious arch to her brow. "And the bean dip?" The subject was food. She would be wise to stick with it.

"Proved successful as a bunion remedy."

"Hmm. I don't suppose the pretzels are safe, then?"

He reached out, took one from her plate and popped it in his mouth, then winced. "Safe, but not recommended." He gently took her plate and set it down on the buffet table, then placed his beside it. "You don't really want to eat, do you?"

His voice was mesmerizing and she found herself awash in the deep, rich timbre of it. "I don't?"

"No."

The single syllable sent shivers down her spine.

"First, you want to dance. And then you want to find a quiet corner and sip champagne and get to know me better."

"I do?" Susannah gulped at the catch in her voice. "I mean, yes, I do," she said in the proper tone.

"Good," he replied.

He grabbed her hand and laced his long fingers through hers. They walked across the room toward the small ensemble. As they passed Lauren and Mitch, she felt both pairs of eyes following their movements. When they arrived at the dance floor, Susannah realized her quest would not be as quick and painless as she had hoped.

"No one's dancing," she said as she stared at the empty expanse of parquet floor.

Jay drew her onto the floor and wrapped his arm around her waist. "We are," he murmured.

He whirled her around, his movements smooth and graceful. To Susannah's mortification, most of the faculty of Wisconsin State stared in disbelief. Obviously dancing was not a normal part of these receptions. Her embarrassment was eased, though, when she realized how easy it would be to get a strand of his hair. But with the warmth of his hand at her waist and the raspy feel of his beard-roughened jaw against her temple, she had to force herself to ignore her reactions to his touch in favor of the task at hand.

She pressed herself closer until her chin rested against his chest, just below his shoulder, and she felt his response, a slight tightening of his hold, a shift of his hips against hers. Suddenly she realized what they were doing. Stage five. Body synchrony. The male and female moving in tandem, a tantalizing prelude to the ultimate act of synchrony—a level that she didn't plan to explore with Jay Beaumont.

Heart pounding, she began a search of the shoulder of his jacket, carefully running her fingers over the fine wool. But she found nothing. Hesitantly she reached up and explored the collar of his crisp striped shirt, but once again, her hand came away empty.

Susannah drew a deep breath, steadying her resolve, then ran her fingers through the silky light-brown hair at his nape. He countered with a soft "hmm"—more than a sigh, but not quite a moan. Clamping her fingers together, she tugged, then carefully pulled her hand away.

She had it! A perfect follicle on a short strand of sun-streaked blond. Jay Beaumont's DNA. Jay turned her gracefully, but in her excitement, the heel of her shoe caught on the side of his and she grasped his shoulder with an open palm. Suddenly, the hair was gone.

Thinking it must have fallen onto the back of his suit, Susannah raised herself on her tiptoes and tried to get a better view. There it was, just below his collar. Another couple danced by and she was surprised to see it was Lauren and Mitch. Her friend shot her a severe look over her partner's shoulder.

What are you doing? her assistant mouthed.

Susannah scowled and pointed to Jay's hair, then resumed her search along his back. Jay stopped suddenly and held her away from him. The music had stopped. The dance was over.

"Why don't you find a quiet corner and I'll get the champagne," he said, brushing her cheek with his knuckles.

With a feeling of panic, she realized Jay was no longer just a disembodied shoulder, clad in navy blue wool. For the length of the dance, she had concentrated on her task. But now, an acutely interested male stood before her and that interest was entirely her fault.

"A-all right. I'll wait for you right over there." Susannah indicated an empty table nestled between the window and a potted palm. He nodded and began to make his way through the crowd to the bar, then turned back to her.

"What's your name?" he asked.

Susannah was momentarily surprised by the question and nearly blurted out her own name. She scrambled to cover her mistake. "Desirée . . . like desire but with an extra *e*."

She groaned inwardly. *Like desire with an extra* e? She wasn't getting better at this, she was getting worse. A blush crept up her cheeks.

"Well, Desire-with-an-extra-*e*, I'm Jay Beaumont."

"It's a pleasure to meet you, Jay," she replied hastily. "I'll just wait for you . . . over there."

She hurried toward the table. The longer she played this game, the harder it was to maintain a cool head. And drooling over Jay Beaumont's astounding good looks wasn't helping her case. She caught Lauren's eye and motioned toward the ladies' room. The line at the bar was long. Long enough to give her time to review her progress with an objective observer and plan her next move.

"SO, WHAT'S she like?"

Jay turned to find Mitch standing beside him at the bar. He grinned and grabbed the chilled bottle of champagne. "Incredibly beautiful and waiting anxiously for me and this champagne."

"Then you'd say she's attractive?"

"Are you blind, Kincaid?"

"Not anymore," Mitch replied with a knowing grin.

"What's that supposed to mean?"

"Remember our little conversation about Dr. Susannah Hart?"

Jay groaned. "Aw, come on, Mitch. Give it up. I don't want to spend a dull evening with some introverted egghead. Not when I've got the delicious Desirée."

"Then you'd better give me that champagne, Beaumont, because you've got an introverted egghead waiting for you right now."

"What are you talking about?"

"That woman you've been lusting after all night is not—what did you call her? Desirée?" Mitch laughed. "Leave it to Susannah to come up with a name like Desirée. That choice of a name just proves my suspicions about what she's doing here."

Jay shot Mitch an annoyed glare. "Give me a clue, Kincaid."

"The woman in the red dress is Susannah Hart. Dr. Susannah Hart."

"*Your* Dr. Hart?"

"One and the same."

"I thought you said she was unattractive."

"I never said that."

"And shy. Any woman who dresses like that is not what I would consider shy. And why is she calling herself 'Desirée'?"

Mitch shrugged. "I'm not exactly sure what's going on, but as near as I can figure, Susannah is doing research."

"She's *what*?"

Mitch chuckled. "And you, Don Juan, are about to become another one of her lab rats."

Jay took a swig of champagne from the bottle and pulled Mitch away from the bar. "Explain yourself, Kincaid," he said tightly.

"Susannah has been involved in some kind of research on sexual response. She hasn't told me about it, but I've managed to piece together a vague idea of what's going on. Her research grant has to do with mud turtles, but I've seen more laboratory rats than mud turtles in her lab."

"So?"

"The lab animals and the books she studies at the library have nothing to do with the mating habits of reptiles. They have everything to do with human sexual response. She's working on something she doesn't want her department head to know about. Believe me, the Susannah Hart I know would never deck herself out as Desirée unless it was in the interests of scientific research."

Jay laughed. "What makes you so sure? She's probably just out for a wild night on the town. All of us have to let loose every now and then. And considering your description of Dr. Hart, I'd say she's probably ready for a little fun. Hey, maybe it's one of those multiple-personality things. You know, scientist by day, seductress by night."

Mitch glared at him. "Not a chance. Besides, when I started questioning Lauren about the lady in red, she became very uncomfortable. Lauren McMahon is definitely in on whatever scheme they're hatching."

"What if you're wrong?" Jay asked.

"I'm not. That's Susannah the scientist you met. And if you don't want to become another one of her research statistics, I think you'd better leave right now."

Jay smiled and took another swig of the champagne. "No way. I'm not leaving, at least not yet. Besides, what harm can she do? If she's into observing human sexual response, she's come to the right place wearing the right dress."

"What are you planning?" Mitch asked.

"I'm just going to have a little fun with our Dr. Desirée. Maybe throw a wrench or two into her research."

Mitch regarded him suspiciously. "And how are you going to do that?"

"First I'm going to get her alone and then I'm going to find out what's going on in that manipulative little mind of hers. I'm going to figure out just what the good doctor is really up to."

"I'm as curious as you are, Jay. But be careful. She's my friend and I don't want to see her hurt."

"You've got nothing to worry about. Just don't let on that we know, okay? And I'll promise to be careful." As careful as a cat in a canary cage, he thought to himself.

"WE'VE PROGRESSED through all five stages," Susannah whispered as she pulled out her notebook. "There's nothing left now . . . except . . . well, *you know*."

"There's a whole lot of business that can be done between now and *you know*, Susannah," Lauren replied. "You can flirt a little, then dance some more. You don't have to contemplate sleeping with the man just to get a strand of his hair! Just play it cool and you'll get what you need."

Susannah looked into the huge mirror that lined one wall of the ladies' room. A wide-eyed stranger stared back at her. That was easy for Lauren to say. The prospect of touching Jay Beaumont again was too much to consider. She imagined her thumb running across his strong lower lip, her palm caressing his cheek, her fingers weaving through his thick, sun-drenched hair. Suddenly she felt dizzy.

Susannah placed her hands on her hot cheeks. Her uncontrolled reaction to Jay Beaumont was born of fear, she rationalized. Fear of being found out, of being revealed as an impostor. There was no way her feelings could be attributed to sexual attraction. All her research proved that attraction was a chemical reaction, an olfactory response to pheromones. The chances of Jay Beaumont possessing the exact pheromone to attract her sexually was slim. He was simply an outstanding male specimen. Genetic imprinting was the cause of this minor lapse into lust, she reasoned, and that could easily be ignored.

"Thank you for occupying Mitch," Susannah said. "But I'm afraid you're going to have to keep him busy a bit longer."

"No problem," Lauren replied. "We're leaving. He's taking me out for pizza."

Susannah sighed. "Lauren, I'm sorry to put you in such an uncomfortable position, but—"

"Don't be silly! Mitch is charming and handsome and really smart. And he's a hunk. Ever since I met him at your office, I've had a little crush on him. He reminds me of Kevin Costner."

Susannah took out a lipstick and retouched her painted lips. "Well, I'm sure you'd much rather be having dinner with your friend, Kevin."

Lauren gave her an odd look, then smiled. "Believe me, Kevin won't mind if I have dinner with Mitch. Kevin and I have a very open relationship."

"If you're certain it's all right." She stared at her reflection, satisfied with the minor repairs to her disguise. "Why don't you go out first and I'll wait here while you and Mitch leave. I don't want to take any further chances of him recognizing me."

Lauren grabbed her hand and gave it a squeeze. "You're doing great, Susannah. Good luck and I'll meet you at the lab tomorrow morning."

I'll need more than luck, she thought as she watched Lauren walk out. She pulled the small bottle of hair spray from her purse and spritzed a generous amount on her fingertips.

A few minutes later, armed with sticky fingers, Susannah left the ladies' room and made her way back to the reception. She found Jay standing beside the small table. He smiled as she approached, then walked toward her. In the next instant, he slipped his arm around her waist and pulled her against his long, lean frame. The breath left her body and she forgot to draw another.

"I thought you'd deserted me," he murmured, staring intently into her eyes.

"I—I just went to the ladies' room," she replied. The arm encircling her waist felt like hot steel, searing and hard. She tried to pull away, but he refused to loosen his hold. Marshaling her resolve again, she reached up to touch his hair. But as suddenly as he grabbed her, he released his hold.

"Let's get out of here," he said.

Susannah nodded mutely.

"My apartment?" he asked.

She nodded again. "I'll meet you there," she said breathlessly. "I have my car here. What's your address?"

He leaned over and whispered the address into her ear. His warm breath teased at her hair. When he drew back, she saw a seductive smile curve his lips. Slowly he moved closer, as if to kiss her. But again, he drew away. "I'll meet you there," he repeated. Then he turned and walked out, leaving her feeling confused and anxious. She tossed the feeling off, grabbed her purse and jacket and followed him out the door.

The drive to his apartment took fifteen minutes. Jay Beaumont lived in a luxurious condo complex built on the river near the edge of town. Susannah had once considered living in the complex, which was noted for attracting single tenants. But she had chosen to put down roots and buy a small bungalow near the campus. The prospect of living amid a crowd of outgoing unmarrieds intimidated her. She preferred a quiet life, spending her free time reading and working in her flower garden.

She sat in the parking lot a full ten minutes before she worked up the courage to walk into the building and ring the bell of Apartment 261. If she kept her cool and played it smart, she could be in and out in less than five minutes. Given Jay Beaumont's ardent attention at the reception, it wouldn't be difficult to get close enough to run her hands through his hair. One kiss, one embrace would be all it would take.

Jay appeared at the door, his suit jacket and tie discarded and his starched blue striped shirt open to the middle of his chest. The crisp fabric molded to the hard contours of his chest and rib cage and tapered to his narrow waist. Susannah's gaze dropped to the open collar of his shirt and she found herself wondering where the dark sprinkling of hair ended. Her fingers tingled with

the need to trace the path and she clenched her fists at her
sides and focused her mind on her objective.

He grabbed her hand and drew her inside. After he
slipped off her jacket, he pulled her over to the couch and
gently pushed her down, handing her a glass of champagne. She sank into the soft leather cushions. But to her
surprise, he didn't join her. Instead he moved across the
room to the breakfast bar and perched on a stool. He
watched her intently.

Susannah sipped at her champagne and waited for him
to speak. When he didn't, she decided to break the silence. "This is a very nice apartment," she said.

"Thank you," he replied in a cool voice. "I like it."

She suffered through another long silence. Susannah
smiled and held up her champagne glass. "The champagne is . . . very nice."

"Hmm." His eyes met hers and she felt as if he could
see right through her. "Tell me about yourself, Desirée.
What do you do for a living? Where do you live? Is your
family from this area?"

Susannah's heart lurched. This was not going at all the
way she had planned. What was she supposed to say?
Desirée was a fraud, a woman who didn't exist. Susannah's mind raced. This strange turn of events called for
drastic action. She stood and put on her most seductive
pose. Then she slowly walked across the room and
shimmied onto the stool next to Jay.

"You don't want to hear about me," she cooed. She
reached up to touch his hair, but he evaded her hand and
stood. He retreated to the other side of the room near the
windows and observed her casually.

"Of course I do. Tell me about your job."

Damn! What was wrong with this man? At this rate,
she'd be running her fingers through his hair sometime

after the turn of the century. Susannah slid from the stool, allowing her short skirt to ride up on her thighs. His gaze fixed on her legs and she saw his reaction in the sharp intake of his breath and a brief flicker of desire in his eyes. She walked past him, her shoulder grazing his chest and her hip brushing against his groin, then stood by the window for a moment before turning around and leaning seductively on the windowsill. Twirling a strand of her hair around her finger, she pursed her lips in a pout. "I don't want to talk about work. I'd much rather concentrate on . . . play." She reached out and ran a finger down the front of his shirt.

Jay frowned and stepped back, just out of her reach. "Would you like more champagne?" he asked.

She shook her head, tossing her hair over her shoulder in an enticing movement. Drastic measures, she thought to herself. She closed her eyes and stretched sinuously, her arms raised over her head. When she opened her eyes he was gone. She glanced around the room in frustration. They seemed to have regressed to the "touch" stage, unable to move any further.

"We're out of champagne," he called from what she assumed was the kitchen. "Would you like a glass of milk?"

Susannah walked into the galley kitchen and smiled in satisfaction. There was barely enough room for one person to maneuver and there was only one way out— past her. She would get a strand of Jay Beaumont's hair here and now.

She stood in front of him and wrapped her arms around his neck. "I don't want a glass of milk," she murmured, reaching for his hair and closing her eyes. "Milk is for children."

Susannah felt a flutter against her chest. The movement skittered along her stomach and then her thighs. Something brushed against her legs, then dropped on her feet.

Susannah opened her eyes with a start, shocked at the liberties Jay Beaumont was taking with his hands. But she was even more shocked to find Jay standing stiffly in front of her, his arms at his side and his eyes directed toward her feet.

She looked down to find her notepad resting against her left foot, open to the page headed with the words "copulatory gaze" in huge capital letters. She stared at it for a long moment, then glanced up to catch Jay's inquisitive expression.

With an mortified smile, she bent down and snatched up the notepad. It was time to either regroup or retreat. "Where is your bathroom?" she asked.

He smiled and pointed down the hall. "Last door on the left."

"Excuse me for a moment," she mumbled. She hurried down the hall and slammed the door behind her, then leaned against it with a heavy sigh. After her heart slowed to its normal rhythm, she began to pace the length of the narrow bathroom, the notepad clutched in her hand.

"What are you doing wrong?" she muttered, glaring at her reflection in the mirror. "You've followed all the steps! But he's gone from hot to cold."

She stopped, leaned over the sink and studied her reflection. "Think!" she commanded. "What next?" It was as if he were deliberately teasing her, thrusting and parrying, evading her touch like a skilled fencer.

Her hand automatically moved to straighten her hair and she reached for her purse, then realized she had left it on the coffee table in the living room. Her eyes scanned the counter and found Jay's brush. She picked it up, brought it to her hair, then froze.

Slowly she lowered the brush and stared at it in realization. His brush! His hair! She ran a fingernail through the bristles and smiled. Without a second thought, she shoved the notepad and Jay Beaumont's brush down the front of her dress.

Jay was standing near the window when she walked back into the living room. He turned and warily watched her approach.

"I have to go now," Susannah said as she snatched up her purse and jacket.

"What?" he said, surprised. "You can't leave now. You just got here." He walked over to her and grabbed her hands.

"Sorry," she said with a smile, pulling from his grasp. She spun around, opened the door and hurried down the stairs. "My husband will wonder where I am," she called over her shoulder.

He followed her into the hall. "Hey, wait a minute. Your hus—"

The front door to his building slammed behind her, cutting off his shout. She ran to her car, got in and locked the door behind her. When her breathing had slowed, she turned the ignition and roared out of the parking lot. She swerved over to the curb several blocks away and pulled the brush from the front of her dress, unable to contain her excitement.

Desirée Smith had served her purpose. She had what she needed for Jay Beaumont's DNA test. Now it was time to put a quick and painless end to the sleazy little hussy and get on with her work. Susannah grabbed a tissue from the glove compartment and wiped as much of the makeup as she could from her face. Then she pulled her hair back and twisted it into a tight knot. She threw Lauren's jacket onto the seat beside her and struggled into her gray wool coat.

From now on, the only woman Jay Beaumont would be attracted to would be plain old Dr. Susannah Hart.

3

SUSANNAH LOVED libraries. From the time she had learned to read when she was four, the library had been a refuge, a safe haven from the constant bickering at home. There was something soothing about the endless shelves of books, the smell of decaying paper and old leather, the peaceful hush and the whispered voices. Libraries felt more like home than any other place on earth, except maybe her laboratory. And Travers Memorial Library, a huge Gothic monstrosity that sat squarely in the center of the campus of Wisconsin State, was by far her favorite.

She stepped through the heavy oak doors and into the softly lit lobby. The sound of her footfalls echoed off the gray stone walls and bounced into the recesses of the high, vaulted ceilings. Tall lead glass windows that diffused the light during the day were now black.

At eight o'clock in the middle of a college weekend, the library was nearly empty, populated by the very few conscientious souls who truly cared about their studies and by those whose first-semester grades foretold the inevitable end to their sojourn in the halls of higher education. That's why she preferred Saturday nights. Most of the students were downtown "cruising the Avenue," visiting the string of college bars that lined both sides of the main street of Riversbend. Tomorrow they would return in great numbers, bleary eyed but filled with scholarly resolve. But tonight the library was hers, and she would revel in anonymity, a humble scholar wandering among the published remains of those who had come before her.

Sometimes she came to the library for no particular reason, just an overwhelming need to feel safe and secure. But tonight she had important work to do. During the past week she and Lauren had spent long hours perfecting the potion formulation based on Jay Beaumont's DNA structure. Three vials of Formulation Number Nine were now finished and awaiting the first field test of their effectiveness—a carefully contrived meeting between Susannah and Mr. Beaumont.

But before she could put her plan into action, she had to prepare. A thorough review of human sexual response was in order, for she would be expected to provide documentation of the results of her experiment and to draw conclusions. She would need to discern the difference between a human male's normal sexual response to stimuli versus the response that her potion triggered. And to this date, most of Susannah's knowledge of males had come from beneath the covers of books rather than beds.

She had been an active participant in only two instances of fully consummated sex. The first had been with a gawky nineteen-year-old physics major after an all-night study group during her third year as an undergrad. She blamed the entire embarrassing affair on a lack of REM sleep. The last had been with an older colleague she'd met at a national symposium held in Miami Beach five years ago. He had been a charming and brilliant man, but when his wife had called in the middle of the night, Susannah had quickly chalked her second sexual experience up to disobedient hormones.

Along the way, there had been other men, but they had
never become lovers. They had been either intimidated
by her intelligence or frustrated by her reticence, and after several dates, to her complete relief, they had quietly
disappeared from her life.

But now, with this experiment, she would have to fend
off the advances of a very magnetic and potent man. Jay
Beaumont was obviously quite experienced in the ways
of the flesh, if the gossip about his personal life was true.
Three women! At the same time! She found the story
difficult to believe, knowing the campus rumor mill's
tendency toward hyperbole. But the tale did cause one
to wonder at the mechanical complications of four people in one bed. And at the sexual stamina of the lone male
in the group.

Her mind flashed an image of the scene: naked limbs
entwined, groping hands and questing mouths in a tangle
of torrid lust. She felt her face grow flushed. The warmth
slowly spread through her body, until her fingers and
toes tingled. Suddenly she felt quite light-headed. An
uncomfortable ache tugged deep within her abdomen
and another vision sprang to life in her mind. Jay Beaumont, alone, standing naked before her in all his masculine glory. A wide, smooth chest tapering to a narrow
waist and slim hips. Strong, finely muscled arms and
gentle, expressive hands. Well-shaped thighs and taut
calves. Her mind wandered back up along his legs to the
true evidence of his maleness.

As a professional, well-versed in anatomy, she knew
the basic proportions one could expect. But this vision
that inhabited her thoughts chose not to conform to the
average. Her fingers clenched instinctively as she imagined touching him there, feeling the silky strength of him
against her palm, holding the soft weight of him in her—

A sharp crack sounded from the conscious realm and Susannah spun around to see a student scrambling to pick up a large volume that had slipped from his grasp and landed flat on the marble floor of the lobby.

How long had she been standing there, staring up at the windows, trapped in her fantasy? How many students or colleagues had passed by, wondering what had prompted the smile that touched her lips or the flush that tinted her cheeks? Susannah stifled a groan as she hurried to the Faculty Services desk. It would be best to pick up the books she had requested and make a quick exit, before she found herself lost in any further lascivious thoughts.

As she approached, she saw a tall figure dressed in faded jeans, tennis shoes and a tan parka, standing at the counter, his back to her. Slightly annoyed, she wondered how long she would have to wait in line behind him. But he seemed preoccupied with flipping through a book as Mrs. Ingrid Severson, the Faculty Services librarian, shuffled through several stacks of volumes next to him. The gray-haired woman looked up and smiled as Susannah placed her bookbag on the counter.

"Well, hello, there. I was wondering when you were going to stop by. I have those books you wanted."

"All of them?" Susannah asked.

Ingrid nodded triumphantly. "I finally found the Ellingson volume in Madison. I had them send it over on interlibrary loan. And strangely enough, I found the Schumacher at the public library in Janesville. You've got it for two weeks before it's due back." Ingrid turned and retrieved a stack of seven books from a shelf behind her and presented them to Susannah.

Susannah slipped her glasses on, grabbed Schumacher's *Gender Roles in Modern Courtship* from the stack and paged through it. "I can't believe you found this. I've looked all over for this book, but it's been out of print for years. You are truly a wonder, Ingrid." Susannah could barely contain her delight as she skimmed through the texts that would help her deal appropriately with Jay Beaumont.

She felt the presence of the other patron beside her and politely moved over to make room for him at the counter. She could sense his gaze on her, but ignored him and moved farther away. *Arousal and Intimacy: A Study of the Sex Drive in American Females*. The title of the top book in her stack nearly filled the cover in big red letters. He moved closer. Maybe he was curious, she thought, still avoiding eye contact. She snatched the book away, only to find the next title even more provoking. *Touch and Taste: Ten Studies in Sensuality.*

Well, he could imagine what he wanted about her reading material, but she wasn't about to be embarrassed! She was a professional and these books were purely professional reading. She waited for him to attempt a witty remark, an opening to conversation, so she could politely rebuff him and continue her discussion with Ingrid. But he didn't speak.

With an irritated sigh, she grabbed the stack of books and tucked them under her arm, then looked up and found Ingrid glancing back and forth between her and the stranger.

"Will there be anything else, Dr. Hart?" Ingrid asked.

"Dr. Hart?" the man asked.

Susannah automatically turned at the sound of his voice, prepared to grace him with one of her withering "I'm not interested" stares. But as his simple query sank into her brain, she froze, her eyes fixed on the man's mouth, unable to move elsewhere. There was no mistaking the rich timbre of that voice or the sexy curl of his mouth as he smiled.

Hesitantly she looked up. But when their gazes met, his smile slowly disappeared into a hard, thin line, as if she herself had somehow transformed before his eyes.

"You!" he said in a near whisper.

Susannah's heart leaped into her throat. He recognized her! But as who? The woman he'd nearly run over with his car? Or Desirée Smith? Her questions were answered almost immediately.

"You're that—that crazy pedestrian! The one who almost totaled my car."

Relief shot through her at his accusation, but her relief was tempered with a growing sense of dread. Unbidden, her brief fantasy came back in full force. A flood of heat warmed her cheeks again, but she controlled her thoughts and focused on the angry man before her. A confrontation with Jay Beaumont was not how she had imagined their next meeting. In fact, any "potionless" conversation with him could prove to be extremely detrimental to the objectivity of her experiment. The consequences of that possibility were too upsetting to consider. An entire week of painstaking work down the drain, never mind her crazy night as Desirée.

Without a reply, she grabbed her bag, quickly thanked Ingrid, then hurried toward the stairs. If she moved swiftly enough, she might manage to lose him in the maze of stacks on the second floor.

"Wait, just one minute," he called in a loud whisper. "I want to talk to you."

She glanced over her shoulder to see him occupied with handing Ingrid his books. Snatching the opportunity, she avoided the main stairs and slipped through the door that led to the library's administrative offices. The hallway was dark, but she had been in this part of the building many times and knew of the ancient elevator at the end of the hall. Once she got to the basement, she could hide out in one of the study cubicles until she was certain he was gone.

She rushed into the elevator, then fumbled with the heavy books. The stack slipped from her grasp and scattered on the floor of the elevator. After she slammed the folding gate of the elevator shut behind her, she hurriedly bent down to retrieve the books before pushing the button marked B. The elevator jerked into action.

There was no one waiting when she stepped out into the lower level of the library, a gloomy, windowless cavern of low ceilings and narrow walkways illuminated by bare light bulbs. She headed to the cubicles that lined one wall of the basement and took the first available space. As far as she could tell, she was alone; there were no other sounds around her.

Susannah threw her bag on the table, dumped her books before her, then sat down and opened a thick volume. Never one to waste time, she would read for a half hour and then find her way back through the stacks to the exit.

For now, her experiment was safe. Tomorrow, she would carefully engineer another meeting with Jay Beaumont. And this time, she would be wearing the potion.

EROTIC FANTASIES of the Twentieth-Century Male. Jay picked up the book from the corner of the tiny elevator and smiled. As he rode the elevator down to the basement level, he casually skimmed the table of contents. The Ménage à Trois Fantasy. The Bondage Fantasy. The Nymphomaniac Fantasy.

Susannah Hart certainly had strange tastes in reading material for one so dedicated to reptile research. A ridiculous image of a leather-clad turtle wielding a whip and handcuffs came to mind, quickly followed by an image of a lizard in lacy lingerie, bearing a cornucopia of sex toys. Jay laughed out loud. Maybe Mitch was right. There was something very strange going on in the brilliant, scientific mind of Dr. Susannah Hart and it had nothing to do with mud turtles.

It had to do with men and women and sex—and his missing hairbrush. Though he couldn't quite figure out where the last came into play in this whole crazy mess.

Jay had spent the past half hour searching the library for her. At first he had just wanted to talk to her, to observe her reaction to him and try to figure out her strange behavior. Her flight from his apartment and her hostile attitude upstairs indicated that she had absolutely no further interest in him. That in itself was odd. Women were normally drawn to him. But he was beginning to realize that Susannah Hart was not a normal woman.

She had wanted something from him, and for all he knew, she had gotten it. Had he been manipulated, been made part of some secret scheme or undercover experiment? If there was one thing he couldn't stand, it was being manipulated by a woman.

There was a time, long ago, when he had trusted women, when he had believed in commitment and devotion. He had met Cynthia when he was home on leave after his second year at the Patuxent Naval Shipyards. His brother, Jack, a naval intelligence officer, had been dating her off and on for nearly a year. The attraction was immediate and for the next month Jay and Cynthia met secretly. Finally they approached Jack and admitted their feelings for each other, and oddly, Jack didn't seem the least bit upset. Later, in private, he merely told Jay to be careful. Jay had thought the comment strange coming from a man who preferred to live life on the edge.

Jay and Cynthia were married in a full military ceremony a month later. For two years, the marriage was perfect, or so Jay thought. Until the day he came home to find Cynthia's closet empty and her bags gone. She had left him a note, admitting to an ongoing affair with his brother. She had never loved Jay, she wrote. She had just hoped to make Jack jealous enough to admit his love for her. Jack Beaumont was spontaneous and adventuresome and she wanted him, not some stuffy naval engineer with dreams of a large family and a house on the Chesapeake.

It took him another two years to recover, and when he did, he threw himself into bachelorhood the same way he threw himself into any other design project, damn the torpedoes, full steam ahead. When his commission was up in the navy, he quit and took over his father's boatyard. Gradually he expanded the business to include naval contracts, and soon after, he diversified. Now Beaumont Industries stood as a testament to his entrepreneurial spirit and Jay Beaumont was wealthy enough to indulge his every whim—including a mansion on the Chesapeake.

On the day Cynthia had walked out, he had made a pact with himself. He would prove her wrong. He would prove that he was more like his brother, Jackson, than she would ever realize. So, conservative Jay Beaumont, family man and devoted husband, slowly transformed himself into Jay Beaumont, confirmed bachelor and all-around ladykiller. And during that wild and wicked metamorphosis, he had learned to know women like the back of this hand.

Maybe that was why he was so determined to get to
the bottom of the mystery that was Susannah Hart. She
was the most puzzling female he'd ever come across. And
for the first time in his recent memory, he found himself
intrigued by a member of the opposite sex.

The elevator came to a stop on the lower level and Jay
stepped out. Slowly he walked along the main aisle,
looking down each row of the floor-to-ceiling shelves on
either side of him. He walked without making a sound,
his tennis shoes silent against the tile floor. As he turned
to search the last narrow aisle, he saw her.

She stood in profile, awash in a circle of white light,
her head bent, a book open in her hands. The bare bulb
created a strange, almost unearthly halo around her head
and shoulders. The dark knot of hair at her nape was
slightly askew and soft tendrils framed her face. On first
meeting he had thought her plain and unremarkable. But
now, under light that would shame most women, he saw
a near-classic beauty. A straight, fine nose. A cupid's-
bow mouth. Mesmerizing eyes hidden behind simple
glasses. And pale, luminous skin that begged to be
touched.

Slowly she flipped a page with a tiny movement of her
finger. Except for that action, she was as still as a dimin-
utive Greek statue, her attention riveted by her reading.
He stood in the shadows for a long while, watching her
and waiting for the right moment to approach.

Then she raised her head and turned his way, as if she
sensed his presence. Her eyes widened as he stepped out
of the shadows. He walked toward her, the book held out
in his hand as a peace offering. She shoved her book back
onto the shelf, then looked to both sides, like a frightened animal. For an instant, she appeared ready to flee,

but then she squared herself to face him in the same indomitable posture she had assumed on the snowy street.

"I believe this is yours," he said quietly.

Hesitantly she took the book from his hand and glanced at the cover. Color rose in her cheeks, heightening her understated beauty even more. She nodded her thanks, then turned and inched along the shelves, pretending to scan the titles.

He moved along with her, not about to let her ditch him again. "I'm afraid we got off to a bad start," he said. "I was hoping maybe we could forget our first meeting and begin fresh. I'll forgive your tendency to jaywalk if you'll forgive my temper. After all, we do have a mutual friend."

Frowning, she stopped and looked at him.

"Mitch Kincaid," he explained.

"Mitch?" she asked in a soft, shaky voice.

It was a small victory, that single word, but a victory nonetheless. He had coaxed her into conversation. Now there was a chance he would learn more about her.

"Mitch and I went to the Naval Academy together. I'm here for a semester as a lecturer in the business school. My name is Jay Beaumont." He held out his hand, but she ignored the gesture, as if touching him might result in serious injury.

"I see," she replied, distrust still evident in her voice.

Jay pulled his hand back. Two words that time. With persistence, maybe he could get an entire sentence complete with multiple clauses before the library closed at midnight.

"Mitch has told me all about you, Dr. Hart. He says you're a biochemist, and a very good one. Is this part of your work?" He pointed to *Erotic Fantasies of the Twentieth-Century Male.*

She shook her head. "No."

Back to one-word replies. He felt as if he were sailing into a strong head wind with a mainsail full of holes.

"Then a hobby, maybe?" His teasing tone did nothing to soften her expression. She really was quite beautiful, in a singular way.

She tipped her chin up. "I'm afraid I don't have time for hobbies."

He grabbed the book from her hand and paged through it. "I can see why. The Dominatrix Fantasy." He held the book up and pointed to the chapter heading. "Not exactly needlepoint, is it?"

She snatched the book back and graced him with a tight smile. "Thank you for returning this. It was a pleasure meeting you, Mr. Beaumont. Please give my regards to Mitch the next time you see him."

She turned to walk away and he reached for her arm. His fingers closed gently over her elbow and she stopped. He was tempted to draw his hand along the length of her limb, to touch the curve of her neck, to caress her face as he had Desirée's. But instead he pulled his hand away, afraid he'd send her running. "Come on, Dr. Hart. Don't be mad at me. I'm really a very nice guy once you get to know me. Ask Mitch, he'll vouch for my character."

Slowly she turned back to him and raised a perfectly arched brow. "And who will vouch for Mitch's character?"

"I'd be happy to," Jay replied. "So, now that we have the character issue resolved, why don't you get your books and your coat and join me for a cup of coffee?"

She shrugged, then turned and began to walk toward the far wall. "I'm afraid I can't, Mr. Beaumont. I have—"

"Jay," he interrupted as she made a quick right through the stacks. He followed her to a long row of study cubicles.

"I have some papers to grade and a lot of reading to do." She carefully gathered the books spread across the table and placed them in a tidy stack.

"But it's Saturday night! No one does schoolwork on Saturday night. Can't it wait until tomorrow?"

She pulled on her coat and buttoned it from bottom to top, then picked up the books. "With that kind of attitude, it's a wonder they let you near college students, Professor Beaumont."

He grabbed the stack of books from her hands and gave her a sexy grin. "If the administration trusts me, maybe you could, too. At least let me carry your books home."

Pulling her bag up on her shoulder, she started toward the elevator at a quick pace. "I'm perfectly capable of carrying my own books," she called over her shoulder. "But if you have a need to engage in a prepubescent male courting ritual, be my guest. My car is parked in the lot." She stepped into the elevator and waited for him to join her. "Well? Are you coming?"

Jay raised his brow and smiled sardonically. "Gee, I'm not sure. Maybe if you promise not to take another swipe at my masculinity, I might be more inclined."

She shot him a patronizing look. "Your masculinity is safe with me, Professor Beaumont. I happen to be quite familiar with the techniques required to feed the male ego." She batted her eyes coyly. "I'm thrilled that you've offered to carry my books and thereby demonstrate your superior strength. Now, get in."

Obeying her firm order, Jay joined her. She pulled the door shut behind him and punched the button for the first floor. He watched her as she kept her eyes focused on the numbered lights beside the door. She shifted uncomfortably, but refused to look at him.

"You remind me of someone," Jay said in a casual, conversational tone.

That brought her gaze back to his in a snap. Bull's-eye. His missile had hit its mark.

"I do?" Her question was laced with suspicion and mistrust. He had her attention now and she was definitely worried, her eyes wide with fear, like a little brown mouse caught beneath a tiger's paw.

"Yes. Someone I met at a faculty reception the other night. You wouldn't happen to have a sister, would you?"

She shook her head vehemently. "I'm an only child."

"A cousin?"

"No!"

The elevator bumped to a stop and she flung the door open and hurried out. Jay had trouble keeping up with her as she raced through the lobby. After waiting impatiently as the guard checked all his books, he finally caught up with her in the parking lot.

She opened her car door and threw her book bag inside, then spun around and grabbed her books from his arms. "Thank you for carrying my books, Professor Beaumont."

"No problem," Jay replied, winded by his hundred-yard dash to the parking lot. "I needed the cardiovascular exercise."

She frowned, oblivious to his sarcasm, then climbed in her car.

"Hey, what about that cup of coffee?" he asked.

"Good night," she said before slamming the door. Seconds later, her car roared out of the half-empty parking lot, leaving Jay standing alone in the dark.

"You can run, but you can't hide," he called out to her taillights. "I'll figure out what you're up to, Dr. Hart. You can count on it."

SCIENCE HALL was silent and dark when Susannah let herself in the back door with her faculty pass key. She didn't need light; she had spent many Saturday nights at work and could find her way to her office and lab blindfolded. Still, the old building was creepy after hours, with its creaking wood floors and its noisy heating system. Susannah felt safer knowing that a security guard prowled the four-story building.

If only she had a security guard to protect her from Jay Beaumont. Their chance meeting at the library had nearly thrown her experiment into a tailspin. Mitch must have mentioned her name to Jay in passing. But there had been no evidence that Mitch had made the connection between Desirée and Susannah. The only thing that worried her now was whether Jay would remain as blind.

A strange pang of jealousy shot through her as she thought of the wanton woman she had created. Jay had been instantly attracted to Desirée and she remembered the sense of power it had given her to lure him, to seduce him. She could still recall the feel of his hard fingers splayed across her back as they'd danced, the shifting of their bodies against each other as they'd searched for perfect synchrony and the luxurious feel of his thick hair slipping through her fingers.

A part of her wished that Desirée could live again, if only to finish the seduction she had started. To drive Jay Beaumont beyond the limits of his self-control and to leave him wanting more. But Desirée had done her job and now it was time for Susannah to do hers.

Susannah turned down the hall that led to her lab. So why was she still attracted to Jay Beaumont? She sighed and shook her head. He was a charming and handsome man, with a wry, self-deprecating humor. A small measure of attraction was only natural. But her feelings for Jay Beaumont were well under control and would have no effect on her experiment.

As she pushed the key into the lock, the door to her lab swung open. Susannah's heart stopped and she stepped back, away from the door. She distinctly remembered locking her lab before she left Friday evening. And Lauren couldn't have forgotten to lock up after herself; she was visiting her parents in Chicago and had left Friday afternoon.

Someone had entered her lab.

She was tempted to call the security guard, but then changed her mind. Maybe the cleaning staff had changed their schedule. Or maybe the guard had opened the door and forgotten to lock it. It would be best to investigate first. Besides, if the individual was still inside her lab, one scream would bring the guard to her aid.

Gathering her courage, she pushed the door open. The hinges squeaked in protest and the glass window clattered as the door bumped against the wall. The light switch was just around the corner. Slowly she crept into the room. A shuffling sound from the far side of the room startled her and she lunged for the switch. Temporarily blinded by the flood of light, she blinked frantically until her eyes adjusted. The sound of a door closing brought her attention to the back corner of the lab.

Each lab was joined to those on either side by connecting doors. To ensure security, the doors had deadbolt locks on both sides and could be opened only by consent of both occupants. Susannah rushed over to the connecting door. The lock on her side was open.

She turned the door knob and tugged, but the door refused to budge. It had been locked from the other side. She drew a shaky breath, flipped the dead bolt, then turned to survey her lab.

At first glance, everything looked in order. The counter that had held Max and Minnie's cage was bare. She had taken the white rats home with her earlier that week and presented them as a gift to the little boy next door. They were both quite tame and would make marvelous pets.

Her gaze darted to the lab cabinet and her pulse quickened. The door was ajar. Susannah hurried over and looked inside. A wave of panic threatened to smother her and she turned and braced her hands on the counter.

The potion was gone!

Closing her eyes, she took a deep, calming breath. Who could have taken it? Whoever it was probably hadn't the slightest idea what they had stolen. She stifled the urge to scream. So much work. It would take them at least two weeks to reformulate the master potion and another week to modify it for Jay Beaumont.

Susannah groaned. Well, she might as well get started now if she hoped to salvage her experiment.

She opened her eyes, then blinked in surprise. A rack of test tubes sat in the middle of the counter in front of her. Three tubes with blue stoppers. Three tubes with the number 9 taped over the stopper. Her potion hadn't been stolen! It had been here, on the counter beside the cabinet, the whole time.

Susannah frowned. But someone *had* taken it out of the cabinet. She was certain she had put the vials away.

She studied the objects on the counter carefully, not wanting to touch anything for fear of disturbing finger-prints, though why she was concerned, she didn't know. She wasn't about to call in campus security or the po-lice. There would be too many questions and a report would be filed with Dr. Curtis and the building chair-person.

Her potion and her secrets were safe. But beyond her relief, she still had a niggling sense that something was not quite right. She just wasn't sure what it was.

Another rack of test tubes stood slightly behind hers and she recognized the lab equipment as Lauren's. The rack held three test tubes, filled with a clear liquid, as hers were. The stopper to one of the tubes lay beside the rack and Susannah reached out to replace it. It was then that she found the damning piece of evidence. Hidden be-hind the rack was a crumpled handkerchief, a clue that pointed to a perpetrator with a chronic case of postnasal drip.

"Derwin," Susannah breathed. A flood of anger coursed through her. She should have known. Professor Curtis had a master key to all the labs and Derwin was clever enough to gain access to the key. "Damn," she muttered. She had underestimated him. On the surface, he appeared to be an irritating fool, but his awkward fa-cade hid a conniving soul. Derwin Erwin had been spy-ing.

But what could he have discovered? The test-tube stoppers were marked with numbers that gave no clue to the contents. And her notes were locked safely in her files. She and Lauren had the only keys. To reassure her-self, Susannah strode to her file cabinet and yanked on each drawer. The cabinet was still locked.

They had been careful about security from the start, and in this instance, it had paid off. She was certain that Derwin had left the lab knowing little more than he had when had he entered.

Susannah returned to the counter and carefully picked up her rack of test tubes. She could take the potion formulation home for safekeeping, but she wouldn't. She'd return the tubes to the cabinet as if they were nothing of importance, and when Derwin made his next covert visit to the lab, he would realize that his spying had been fruitless.

And on Monday, her experiment would proceed as if nothing had happened. She would dab the potion on her pulse points and set off across campus to bump into Jay Beaumont. A tiny thrill shot through her.

If all went as planned, Jay Beaumont would soon be madly in love with Dr. Susannah Hart. And Dr. Susannah Hart would be well on the way to securing a place in the annals of science.

4

"THAT SNEAKY, spineless, mutant *Blattid!*"

"*Blattid?*" Susannah asked, watching her lab assistant pace the narrow width of her office. "Derwin is a water bug?"

"Cockroach," Lauren muttered.

"Old Derwin's definitely moving in the wrong direction on the food chain," Susannah joked in an attempt to lighten Lauren's mood. "I can't believe I'd forgotten that one. Water bugs are *Belostomatids*. That same problem cost me a perfect grade in my undergraduate—"

Lauren stopped her pacing. "Susannah! Aren't you even the least bit angry about this? Derwin snuck in here Friday night and messed with your research."

"*Our* research," she corrected, folding her hands in front of her. Her outward show of calm had no effect on Lauren's temper. "What's done is done. He tampered with your rack of test tubes, as well," she added.

"My research?" The heightened color in Lauren's cheeks slowly drained away along with her anger. "He was messing with my research? My potion formulations?"

Susannah shook her head in confusion at Lauren's sudden shift in behavior. "*Your* research? You mean *our* research."

Lauren smiled uncomfortably, then sat down in a chair in front of Susannah's neatly kept desk. "Right," she quickly replied. "Our research."

"Besides, it didn't look like he had seriously tampered with anything. One of your test tubes was missing a stopper, but that's all." Susannah studied her assistant's guilty expression and Lauren dropped her gaze to her hands, where she examined her fingernails a bit too intently. "Are you working on something you're not telling me about?"

"Why would you ask that?"

"Because of that look on your face." Lauren remained silent and Susannah sighed. "I've always encouraged you to pursue whatever work makes you happy. You'll get your doctorate in another year and then you'll be leaving to begin your own research. Just because you're working with me doesn't mean you have to push aside your own interests."

Susannah could understand Lauren's need for secrecy. She had her own set of secret motivations for her experiments. Though she tried to deny it at first, she had come to the conclusion early on that her obsession with pheromone research had a great deal to do with her childhood. Divorce had torn her family apart when she was eight and from that moment on, Susannah had searched for answers. Her father, a well-respected surgeon, had remarried and divorced again before Susannah had graduated from high school at age sixteen. And her socialite mother had collected three wealthy exhusbands by the time her twenty-five-year-old daughter had graduated summa cum laude with her doctorate in biochemistry.

For a long time, Susannah had blamed herself. An only child, she was plain and introverted and a far cry from the beautiful social butterfly her mother was determined to mold. And her father? He could not forgive Susannah for having been born female. Even though she'd thrown herself into her studies, determined to show him that a woman could become as fine a doctor as a man, he had still left.

How ironic that his daughter was now on the verge of a discovery that could have saved Spencer Hart thousands of dollars in divorce settlements, a discovery that could have saved her parents' marriage and preserved her family. But the past was past. The divorce had happened more than twenty-five years ago. And the only comfort she would find now was in the fact that her potion might protect the childhood of some other frightened eight-year-old girl whose parents refused to get along.

"When you decide to tell me about whatever it is you're working on, I'll be ready to listen," Susannah said.

"Thanks," Lauren said with a grateful sigh. "And I promise, we'll discuss it as soon as I get some of the kinks worked out. I really need to try this on my own."

Susannah straightened a stack of papers, then put them into a file folder. "By the way, I ran into Jay Beaumont at the library on Friday night," she said, trying to sound nonchalant.

Lauren's eyes widened and she moved to the edge of her chair to rest her elbows on Susannah's desk. "You didn't! What happened? Did he recognize you?"

"Only as the woman who almost wrecked his car," Susannah replied with a casual shrug. "I tried to avoid contact as best I could. I didn't want to skew the results of our field test one way or the other. But after some initial hostility, he seemed determined to smooth things out between us. It seems he's a good friend of Mitch Kincaid's."

Lauren's expression lit up like a thousand-watt light bulb. "I know. He and Mitch were roommates at the Naval Academy. He's got the longest eyelashes I've ever seen."

"Jay?" Susannah asked, perplexed.

Lauren shook her head. "No, Mitch. He's writing a book on the history of naval engineering."

"Mitch is writing a book on naval engineering?"

Lauren gave her an impatient look. "No, Jay! Mitch says that Jay is incredibly smart and that his book will probably be the definitive text on the subject. And Mitch says that—"

Susannah raised an eyebrow and Lauren stopped in midsentence. "Limerence," Susannah stated.

"What?" Lauren gasped.

"You heard me and don't play dumb. Limerence. A state of frenzied infatuation. Dorothy Tennov?"

Lauren looked at her, shocked. "I know the source. I researched it for you," she answered, her voice faltering. Suddenly she groaned and buried her face in her hands. "Oh, God. Does it show?"

"Your face is flushed, your hands are trembling and you're babbling like a lovestruck teenager. You're infatuated with Mitch Kincaid!"

Lauren looked up and gave Susannah a wavering smile. "You don't mind, do you? I mean, I know he's your friend, but you've never mentioned having any romantic inclinations toward him. If this bothers you, I'll stop seeing him."

Susannah opened her mouth to reassure Lauren, then stopped. How *did* she feel? Was the small shard of pain that pierced her heart jealousy? Or was it envy? Susannah had no romantic designs on Mitch Kincaid; he was simply a good friend, a friend she should want to see happy. And what better woman for Mitch than Lauren, her best friend?

Still, she couldn't help but feel a bit envious. She envied Lauren's bright, hopeful expression, her breathless anticipation and her unquenchable optimism. Lauren was feeling elation so deep that it seemed to transform her very soul until she shimmered with repressed excitement. She was no longer alone. She had chosen a partner in an age-old dance, a dance to which Susannah would never be invited. Lauren believed in love. Susannah didn't.

"Of course I don't mind!" Susannah replied, grabbing Lauren's hand and giving it a squeeze. "I think it's wonderful. How does Mitch feel?"

Lauren laughed. "I think he's as loony as I am. When I'm not with him, all I do is think about him. And when I'm with him, I can barely speak. We've seen each other nearly every night since the reception. I wanted to tell you, but I wasn't sure how you'd feel. When I went home this weekend for my dad's birthday, I gave him my parents' phone number so he could call me. He lost the number and called every McMahon in the Chicago directory in alphabetical order until he found the right one. Luckily my dad's name is David. Can you believe it?"

"What?" Susannah teased. "That your dad's name is David?"

"No, that Mitch spent three hours on the phone before he got me."

"It's the phenylethylamine," Susannah answered logically. "All these feelings of euphoria and elation are simply caused by chemical and electrical reactions in the limbic system of the brain. It's like a shot of amphetamine. Mitch probably would have continued calling until the effects of the PEA wore off."

"Susannah, this is love, not a laboratory experiment! I can't get him out of my mind."

She nodded in understanding. Classic symptoms. Odd, though, that Lauren couldn't recognize them on her own. "That's because your cortex combines these limbic-system emotions with constant thoughts of each other. Electrical impulses are traveling through your neurons and hopping across your synapses and with all the PEA flooding your nerve cells, your brain probably resembles the residential electrical system of New York City right about now." She must remember to record Lauren's behaviors and compare them with the published research. Lauren's reactions might prove to be very useful to her field data.

Lauren was silent as she stared at Susannah, an incredulous expression fixed on her face. "That's a textbook answer. Are you saying that you really don't believe in love? Even just a little?"

Susannah jumped to answer, but then stopped herself. How she wanted to say yes, to say that she too had experienced the depth of emotion that Lauren was feeling now. But it would be a lie. She had never really admitted her convictions out loud, though by her research she assumed they were obvious. "Only as a chemical reaction. You know that."

"Well, I prefer to take the romantic side of this argument. You can have the chemical side. I'd still rather think of love in totally impractical and unscientific terms, even though I'm spending my days trying to prove otherwise."

Susannah stood and efficiently arranged a stack of file folders. "We'll prove that love *is* chemical. I have no doubt about that. The potion is ready, I've finished all my reading and it's time to get to work. The only problem I've got now is trying to figure out where to find Jay Beaumont."

"I could call Mitch," Lauren offered, a moony look in her eyes. "He would know." She paused. "He knows everything."

"Not a chance. Even though he would probably be so enamored by the sound of your voice, he still might wonder why you're asking."

"You're probably right," Lauren agreed. "I could call Lisa at the business school. I'll bet she has access to the faculty schedules. You could wait around after one of his classes and casually bump into him."

"Hmmm. That would work. We can trust your friend, can't we?"

Lauren nodded. "Definitely. I'll get right on it."

While Lauren made her phone call, Susannah hurried to the ladies' room, a vial of the potion tucked in her jacket pocket. As she stood before the mirror, she examined her reflection. Then she pulled off her glasses and looked more closely at her features. Still plain and unremarkable. Her stint as Desirée had done nothing to change that. She put her glasses back on. It was important to appear as bland and uninteresting as possible. She was dressed in gray again today, in a muted herringbone tweed jacket and a simple skirt. Jay Beaumont's attention would not be drawn to a beautiful face or colorful clothing. His attention would be drawn by the potion or not at all.

She uncorked the test tube and tipped it against her index finger, then touched the liquid to her pulse points — behind each ear, at the base of her neck and a dab on each wrist. For good measure, she moistened her fingertips

with the potion, then ran them across her tightly bound
hair and brushed a drop on each temple. By the time
she'd tucked the vial into her pocket, her heart was rac-
ing and her breathing was erratic.

She and Jay Beaumont would meet again. The thought
caused another rush of nervousness as she remembered
their previous meetings and her strange response to his
presence. A sudden longing for his touch nearly overwhelmed her and she crossed her arms and rubbed her
upper arms furiously to stop a shiver. Though she had
searched for an explanation for her reactions time and
time again over the past few days, none had been forth-
coming. If she didn't know better, she would have to admit that her damp palms and muddled mind were
symptomatic. But of what?

Maybe stress, she rationalized. Or possibly she was
coming down with a mild influenza. Another excuse
skittered through her mind. No! Certainly not limerence! She was not, repeat not, infatuated with Jay Beaumont. The idea was too absurd even to consider. Most
likely, it was simply a side effect of wearing the potion.
That was it. She would have to take careful note of this
during the experiment and make adjustments accord-
ingly.

Satisfied, Susannah gathered her resolve and shored
up her defenses. If the potion worked, his attraction to
her would be instant and undeniable. Jay would pursue
her with a single-minded purpose and the chase would
be on. She had no choice but to run. Though she knew
that playing "hard to get" would only intensify his desire, she also knew that the lust would have to remain
one-sided. She would see to that.

With that resolution in mind, she exited the ladies'
room. As she hurriedly rounded the corner of the hall-

way that led back to her office, she was brought to a stop
by a tall figure and a near collision.

She looked up from the front of a T-shirt emblazoned
with a picture of a skull, two guitars and the saying
"Rock 'Til U Drop" and into the beady eyes of Derwin
Erwin. A flutter of fear crossed his features before he
forced a smile. She felt an immediate sense of satisfaction at his anxiety. Her suspicions were right; Derwin had
entered her lab. There was no doubt about it now.

"Dr. Hart," he said with a nod.

"Mr. Erwin," Susannah replied coolly.

She moved to her left to pass by, at the same time Derwin did, and they nearly collided again. A move to her
right resulted in the same. Finally, she shot him a quell-
ing look and he froze, ending their bizarre cha-cha.
Though she was tempted to accuse him then and there,
she held her temper. It would do no good to cause a
scene, so she stepped around him and continued briskly
down the hall.

"Dr. Hart?"

Derwin's words echoed through the silence. Susannah stopped, then turned to find him standing in the
middle of the hall with a dopey look on his face, his
hands twisting at the front of his baggy T-shirt.

"What is it?" she asked impatiently.

"You—you look...ah, extremely..." He drew out his
handkerchief and wiped at his nose. "What I meant to
say was, you look lovely today, Dr.... Susannah."

He grinned at her and Susannah felt a small measure
of revulsion. Cockroaches didn't smile, but if they did,
she was certain they would resemble Derwin at this moment. What was this all about, this sudden compliment? Was the little bug trying to get back in her good

graces after his thwarted attempt at academic espionage? Was he afraid she would report him to Dr. Curtis?

"Would you care to explain yourself, Mr. Erwin," she said, her tone cold and commanding. She strode back to him and gave him a stare to match the subzero temperature of her words. But as she faced him, five-foot-four of righteous indignation, Derwin seemed unfazed. The dumb, slack-jawed look remained.

"It's just that I—I never noticed how—how lovely your hair is," he gushed. "It reminds me of—of—dirt. It's the exact color of—dirt. Sort of—brown. Youlookveryalluringtoday." The last came out in an almost unintelligible, uncontrollable rush.

Susannah knew she should have felt raging anger, but she found herself as dumbfounded as Derwin seemed to be. She had expected an excuse for the break-in to her lab, not a backhanded compliment. Upon further study of his expression, she realized that there was no trace of insincerity in his words. He truly meant what he had said.

With an edgy gesture, she smoothed her hair back and Derwin's gaze followed her fingers longingly. Drawn by his odd reaction, she tugged at the cuff of her jacket and his eyes shifted to stare at that movement. Slowly she moved her hand between her hair and her cuff and back again, and Derwin's gaze bobbed up and down like a judge at a trampoline championship. Susannah touched her right shoulder and then her left, back and forth, and his rapt attention to her fingers still didn't waver.

She clenched her teeth and bit back a rising flood of frustration. Just what was Derwin Erwin up to? His behavior was beyond appropriate. Did he think she was so desperate for a man that she would ignore his treachery in favor of his feeble attempt at a compliment? Impatiently she snapped her fingers in front of his nose and his trancelike stare shattered.

"I have work to do, Mr. Erwin," she said, raising her voice to be clearly understood and poking a sharp finger into his chest. "And so do you. I'd suggest you get to it."

With that, Susannah walked down the hall and into her office. When she got inside, she backed up against the wall next to the door. Thirty seconds later she could still hear his sniffling in the hall. Derwin continued to linger for another two minutes before she heard him turn and amble toward Dr. Curtis's office.

Susannah could only theorize that he had taken an overdose of the nasal inhalant he was perpetually sniffing and was suffering mild hallucinations.

Ten minutes later she was headed across campus, a copy of Jay Beaumont's class schedule in one pocket and a vial of potion in the other. Her strange encounter with Derwin forgotten, she had but one person on her mind. There was no turning back now. Jay Beaumont was about to fall head over heels in love with her.

But by midafternoon when she returned to her office, Susannah was thoroughly frustrated, her body battered and nearly frozen to the bone. At 10:05 a.m., she had watched Jay Beaumont leave his office as she bent over the water fountain in the hallway outside. He had walked right by without noticing her. Hurrying after him, she had raced to his next stop, an undergraduate marketing class at Parker Hall. But on the way she twisted her ankle on a cracked sidewalk, fell down and skinned her knee, and had limped up the steps ten minutes after his class began.

She had waited around in the overwarm lobby and at 11:10 a.m., Jay exited the lecture hall, surrounded by a crowd of students. She had tried to approach, getting within five feet of him, but he was deep in conversation and showed no indication that he had seen her. Once again, she had discreetly followed him across campus, back to his office, where he held office hours until lunch.

A brief trip to the vending machine for a soothing cup of coffee had caused her to lose track of him again. When she returned to the hallway outside his office, the line of students had disappeared and so had Jay Beaumont. Lisa's information stated that he often visited the swimming pool during his lunch hour, so Susannah had struck out for the far end of campus. As she had stood at the curb waiting to cross the street, a car had sped by, splashing slush over her feet and the front of her coat.

At 12:15 p.m., she had dragged herself, along with her swollen ankle, scraped knee, sloshing shoes and muddy coat, up the stairs to the observation deck above the pool. There she had watched Jay swim laps for what seemed like hours. Back and forth, from one end of the pool to the other, he sliced through the water, first the breast stroke, then a crawl, followed by the butterfly and then the backstroke.

Transfixed by the sight of his lean, muscular body dressed only in brief, body-hugging trunks, Susannah had left the observation deck to get a closer look poolside. But when she had reached the wall of windows that lined one side of the pool, he had been gone. She had waited in the lobby for more than thirty minutes, nearly giving up, when Jay strode out of the locker room with Mitch Kincaid at his side. Laughing, they had breezed right past her hiding place behind a pillar. Just before Jay exited through the glass doors, he had stopped and looked back into the lobby, but Susannah had been quick enough to dart behind the pillar before he caught sight of her.

She had spent the next half hour outside, on the Student Union Commons, where Jay and Mitch bought hot dogs from a outdoor vendor and sat down on a concrete bench to eat them. Though the temperature was above freezing and most of the snow had melted the day before, a damp wind had roared between the buildings, buffeting her until her fingers and toes were numb and her cheeks raw with the cold. Jay and Mitch had chosen a sunny spot, sheltered from the wind by a building, oblivious to her plight. Finally, unable to take the cold any longer, Susannah had stumbled stiffly back to her office, arriving at 2:14 p.m.

By 2:15 p.m., she had wiped every trace of the potion away, torn Jay Beaumont's class schedule to bits, thrown both her soggy shoes at an ancient bust of Louis Pasteur, swept a pile of file folders off her desk and across the floor of her office and tossed three of Dr. Louisa Gruber's books into the trash can from a range of six feet, the last with an admirable bank shot off the radiator.

Exhausted, Susannah sank into her chair, crossed her arms on her desk and lowered her head. The afternoon had been a complete failure. She hadn't made contact and was no closer to learning of the potion's effectiveness than she had been this morning.

Nothing was going as she had planned! Scientific experiments were supposed to proceed in an orderly, logical manner; that was the way things were done. But unlike a proper scientific subject, Jay Beaumont did not act and react as expected. In fact, nothing he did or said could be predicted. She would have to gain control of this situation, or risk blowing three years of painstaking work.

THERE IS NOTHING quite so pathetic as a man obsessed with a woman, Jay thought wryly. He had been obsessed once, a long time ago. But after Cynthia's desertion, he had made a solemn vow never to allow a woman to control any facet of his life. He had kept that vow. Until today.

Now, standing in the hallway outside Laboratory 107 in Science Hall, Jay couldn't even work up a decent case of self-loathing. Instead, he had good cause to revise his opinion of those poor souls caught in the clutches of a manipulative female. After all, there were times when a man just had to say, "To hell with it all," and let instinct take over.

Since he had stepped out of his office earlier that morning, thoughts of Susannah Hart had dogged him wherever he went. Her image drifted in and out of his mind until, as if by sheer force of will, she had appeared. He thought he saw her outside his marketing class, but when he glanced in her direction she was gone. He was certain he saw her on the observation deck, watching him swim laps. And then she was gone again, as if she had vanished into thin air. As he was leaving the building, he had felt a strange sensation of being observed and turned to see her dart behind a concrete pillar. He saw her once more, outside the Student Union, while he and Mitch were eating lunch.

At first he thought the sightings were simply delusions, a side effect of his celibate life-style. Considering he was fixating on a woman who wanted nothing to do with him, it was a plausible explanation. But by the end of the afternoon, he had convinced himself that he wasn't going over the edge. Susannah Hart had been secretly following him, and doing a damn poor job of it.

What the hell was she up to? And more to the point, why the hell did he care? Mitch had claimed she was involved in research on sexual attraction. More like research in avoiding him, he thought. They had met only three times and in each of those cases their encounter had ended with the elusive Dr. Hart running out on him.

He could understand her taking off after the accident. His temper didn't invite polite conversation. And at his apartment, she had probably just lost her nerve and realized she'd taken a wild night on the town a little too far. But at the library, she had made her feelings clear. She wanted nothing to do with him. Jay was not one to waste time on an unwilling female, especially one as balmy as Susannah Hart. Not when there were easier, and saner, options available.

So what was he doing standing outside her lab? What had drawn him there against his own common sense? Whatever power Susannah Hart held over him, he was determined to end it here and now. There was no way he was going to let some looney scientist get under his skin.

Jay raised his hand to rap at the door, then stopped in midmotion. It might be better to use the element of surprise, to catch Dr. Hart off guard. He reached for the doorknob, then considered the benefits of slipping into her lab silently versus the benefits of bursting through the door in a fit of anger. While he weighed his choices, the doorknob turned and the door swung inward.

He watched as Susannah Hart moved toward him, her arms clutching a stack of file folders and her nose buried in the contents of the top folder. In a single instant, he absorbed the sight of her, her features flooding his mind and seeping into every corner of his parched soul. How was it that his memories of her never quite did justice to her beauty?

Her glasses were perched on the end of her nose, and over the tops of the rims he glimpsed long, thick lashes ringing eyes that tipped up slightly at the corners. Her deep russet hair, though bound at her nape, curled in unruly tendrils around her face, caressing a flawless complexion. A pencil was tucked behind her left ear and she held another between her full lips. A white lab coat covered, but did not hide, her feminine curves.

Jay found himself unable to move, unable to step out of her way, and a moment later she slammed into his chest. He reached down to grab her arms and steady her, and when she looked up, her brown eyes widened into saucers of surprise.

"Wub are oo gooing ear?" she asked after a long silence, the pencil still trapped firmly between her teeth.

Jay reluctantly released one warm, soft arm and reached over to pull the pencil from her mouth. "Do you *ever* watch where you're going, Dr. Hart?"

She stared at him in disbelief. "You're here," she breathed.

Jay smiled sardonically. "It would appear that way now, wouldn't it?"

"But—but why are you here?" she asked, openly curious. "I—I mean what brings you over to this side of campus, Mr. Beaumont?"

"I was hoping you might be able to enlighten me, Dr. Hart."

A glimmer of apprehension colored her expression and she ran her tongue across her upper lip nervously, a quirk suggestively reminiscent of Desirée.

"Do you mind if we speak somewhere more private?" he asked. She glanced hesitantly over her shoulder to indicate the lab. With that, Jay turned her around and steered her back inside, then kicked the door closed behind them. Susannah jumped slightly when the door slammed, and pulled out of his grasp to retreat to the far side of the room.

"Was there something you wanted, Mr. Beaumont?"

There was a lot that he wanted, he thought to himself. Explanations topped the list. And he wanted that challenging look to disappear from her eyes. He wanted her to smile at him and touch him the way she had when she was Desirée. And most of all, he wanted to pull the pins from her hair and run his fingers through the silky weight of it. He wanted to yank off her lab coat—

Jay swallowed hard. "Yeah, there's something I want. I want to know why you were following me around campus."

Susannah spun away from him and busied herself with arranging her file folders on the counter. "Following you?" she asked over her shoulder. "Why would I be following you?"

Jay casually walked across the room and braced his hands on either side of her. He leaned over, barely brushing her slender back with his chest, and inhaled the indescribably tantalizing scent that was Susannah Hart. "You tell me, Dr. Hart," he whispered into her ear.

Susannah slowly turned to face him, pressing her body into the counter to avoid touching him. As she moved, her hip brushed against his groin, and he felt his blood race to the general vicinity of his lap. She stood just inches away, watching him warily, and he was sorely tempted to pull her into his arms and kiss her, to span her narrow hips with his hands and drag her against his aching need.

Jay's jaw tightened. What the hell was he doing? He was here to find out what Susannah Hart was up to, not to seduce her.

"Give me one good reason why I would follow you around campus," she said, her voice choked.

Jay stepped back, regaining control. "Maybe you wanted to apologize," he muttered.

"Apologize? For what?"

"For nearly wrecking my car?"

She smiled nervously, avoiding his probing gaze. "I thought we'd agreed to put that incident in the past, Mr. Beaumont."

"Jay," he insisted, dipping his head to catch her eyes. Lord, she had incredible eyes, mesmerizing, yet filled with innocence. He could live forever in those eyes. "How about for your rude behavior at the library?"

She stiffened and shot him a defiant look. "Rude? I was not rude! I was simply... preoccupied."

Jay felt another magnetic pulse race through his body and he moved closer and bent his head. His lips were just inches from hers; he could feel the gentle flutter of her breath against his cheek. Without warning, she slid down against the counter and under his outstretched arms. Once again, she retreated to the other side of the room and watched him distrustfully.

Jay shrugged, leaned against the counter and crossed his arms in front of him. "Usually when a boy carries a girl's books for her, she reciprocates by agreeing to accompany him to the local malt shop for a soda."

"We're not children, Mr. Beaumont."

"I'm well aware of that, Susannah. So, we'll find an adult equivalent to the malt shop. How about dinner Saturday evening at the Canterbury Inn?"

She hesitated before answering, once again avoiding his gaze. "I'm sure there are plenty of other women who would love to go out to dinner with you. Why not ask one of them?"

He slowly crossed the room to stand before her. "I want to go out with you," he replied.

"Why?"

"Funny. I've asked myself that same question."

"And what was the answer?"

"Why not?" he teased.

She looked up at him impatiently. "Are you always this obtuse?"

"No," he replied with a laugh. "Are you always this evasive?"

"No," she answered stubbornly.

He tipped her chin up with his finger until she was staring into his eyes. "Good," he murmured. "Then we'll have plenty to talk about over dinner, won't we?"

She nodded, her gaze trapped by his, her soft lips parted slightly. Again he bent toward her, hoping to take just a small taste of what she offered. This time she didn't move away, just stood paralyzed, her breathing shallow and erratic. He spread his palm across the smooth angle of her jaw. She moaned softly and in the background he heard the door open, but Jay was too far gone to pull back. He wanted—no needed—to taste her, to learn if she was as sweet as he had imagined.

"Get your scummy hands off her, you despicable cad!"

Susannah jumped, pushing against his chest with her palms, and Jay muttered a curse. Slowly he straightened, his jaw tense, and turned to face the door, slipping his arm protectively around Susannah's waist.

A tall, skinny kid stood in the doorway, his pubescent complexion mottled with anger, his fists clenched. "Unhand her this moment," he demanded, his voice cracking on the last word.

"Derwin! What are you doing here?" Susannah gasped, a rising blush coloring her cheeks.

"Derwin?" Jay asked.

"Derwin Erwin. Graduate assistant to my department head," Susannah whispered.

"I'm saving you from this . . . this giggle-oh!" Derwin stated boldly.

"Gigolo," she corrected. "I don't know what's gotten into him," she explained to Jay in hushed tones.

"Gigolo?" Derwin asked.

"Yes," she confirmed impatiently.

"Like I said, unhand her this instant, you . . . you gigolo!" He shook his fist in Jay's direction.

"What would you like me to do?" Jay whispered to Susannah.

She shrugged. "I have no idea."

Jay released Susannah and ambled toward Derwin, trying to add a measure of menace to his movements. Though the kid was several inches taller, Jay had at least thirty pounds and considerable muscle over him. "Gigolo? Is that what you called me, Erwin?"

Derwin nodded defiantly.

"I'll have to take that as a direct insult to my character," Jay said dryly, "and to the unquestionable moral standards of Dr. Hart. What do you say, Erwin?" He came face to face with him, staring him down like a prizefighter bent on intimidation. "Pistols at dawn?"

Derwin swallowed convulsively, his Adam's apple bobbing up and down under his pointed chin. "I—I—"

"You'd better leave while you still have all your teeth, Erwin," Jay said in a deceptively even voice, quiet enough to keep his threat from carrying to Susannah.

Derwin looked frantically back and forth between Susannah and Jay, before he nodded in defeat and backed toward the door. "I—I was just trying to protect her," he mumbled.

"She has all the protection she needs right now," Jay answered as Derwin skulked out.

With a satisfied grin, Jay turned back to Susannah. "What was that all about?"

She shook her head in confusion, her eyes wide. "I haven't a clue." Susannah crossed the room and peeked out into the hallway, then slowly closed the door and turned to face Jay.

"Your honor has been upheld, fair lady," Jay teased, bowing before her. "And now you must bestow a favor on your brave and noble knight."

A giggle burst from Susannah's throat, the musical sound surprising Jay as much as it seemed to surprise her.

"Brave?" she scoffed. "Noble? Derwin is frightened of the nose on his own face."

"I can see why," Jay countered.

Susannah smiled. "You know what I mean. You could have said 'Boo!' and sent him running faster than a bright light clears a room full of *blattids*."

"Blattids?"

"Cockroaches," Susannah answered informatively.

"A vivid allusion," he muttered. How had they moved from kissing to cockroaches? "So what do you think?" he asked, hoping to get her back on subject.

"I've always considered the cockroach an amazing insect. It's a very tenacious and resilient species. Did you know that—"

"I meant about dinner," Jay interrupted.

She looked up at him, surprised by the turn in conversation. "Dinner?"

"The Canterbury Inn, Saturday evening. I'll pick you up around seven? And don't ask me why, just say yes."

She hesitated for a moment, then nodded. "All right."

Her indecision was obvious and it caused a brief flare of irritation. She managed more enthusiasm discussing cockroaches than dinner with him. Even so, they had reached a milestone of sorts. Susannah Hart had agreed to a date. Given an evening alone with her, Jay was certain he'd be able to discover the reasons behind her strange behavior toward him . . . and his toward her.

He grabbed her hand and brought it to his lips, brushing a gentle kiss across her knuckles. Her gaze followed his every movement. "Saturday night, then."

She smiled haltingly, her eyes locked with his, then nodded.

With that, he walked to the door, then stopped and turned toward her. In three short strides he was back in front of her, his arm wrapped firmly around her waist. His mouth came down on hers and he kissed her, recklessly and thoroughly. Then he stepped away and looked down into her flushed features.

Slowly she opened her eyes and stared up at him in astonishment.

He tried to control his own shock at his impulsive behavior. What had possessed him to kiss her? They barely knew each other. "I don't know why I did that," he said apologetically. "But I'm glad I did," he added with a grin.

She nodded her agreement.

"Susannah?"

"Yes . . . Jay?" she said, a bit breathlessly.

"I'll see you on Saturday night. And promise me you'll leave the bug talk in the lab." Without waiting for an answer, he spun on his heel and strode down the hall.

Jay smiled to himself. Dinner with Susannah Hart promised to be a very interesting and enlightening evening.

5

"OH, MY!" The exclamation escaped as a soft whisper.
Susannah placed her fingertips on her lips in an attempt
to brush away the tingling sensation that had rendered
two-syllable words impossible. But to her surprise, her
fingers came away similarly affected. She shook her
hand, trying to restore the feeling. Dazed, she pushed the
door of her lab shut and walked to the counter on rub-
bery legs.

What was wrong with her? Her entire body was now
affected by this strange neurophysical malady. She rum-
maged through a cabinet and came up with a foot-long
lab thermometer, then slipped it under her tongue. Her
face felt flushed and her pulse was pounding through her
head like a herd of *elephas maximi*. Influenza—that had
to be it, or the beginnings of a full-blown head cold.
Placing her palm on her forehead, she searched for signs
of a fever. Though she felt hyperpyretic, her forehead
was cool to the touch. Groaning, she pulled the thermometer from her mouth and placed it on the counter.

Why make excuses? Just who was she kidding? She
knew the signs and symptoms. She didn't have the flu—
she had a bad case of Jay Beaumont. A case she had
caught the instant he had walked into her lab.

The thought of his lips against hers brought another
feverish rush and Susannah slid onto a lab stool before
she completely lost her ability to stand. She was exhausted and energized all at once. She found herself

craving more: a deeper kiss, a closer embrace, a more intimate exploration. How would it feel to have his hands take control of her body, to lose herself to the incredible sensations of being touched by him? Suddenly she desperately wanted to know.

No! This wasn't supposed to happen! Jay Beaumont was her research subject and she was a scientist who knew better than to get personally involved in an experiment. The problem was, Jay was much harder to ignore than a mating mud turtle.

So what was causing this odd attraction? *Could* Jay Beaumont possess the exact pheromone necessary to attract her? The odds of that happening were astronomical, to say the least. Susannah pushed the idea away immediately. She didn't believe in fate any more than she believed in love.

Whatever it was, she would have to get control of herself. She had already made a muddle of her first attempt to field-test the potion. At least she would have another chance. Dinner with Jay Beaumont was more than she deserved after such an unqualified scientific failure.

The door to the lab opened and Susannah looked up idly as Lauren walked in. When Lauren caught sight of her morose expression, she smiled sympathetically.

"Don't tell me," she said. "It didn't work?"

"What?" Susannah asked, still occupied with thoughts of Jay Beaumont and her mutinous reaction to him.

"The potion didn't attract Jay Beaumont?"

"Not exactly," Susannah murmured.

"What happened?"

She related her futile attempts to bump into Jay, and by the end of her story Lauren was having a hard time containing her amusement.

"It's not funny!" Susannah cried. "When he showed up here, I made a total fool of myself. I was so upset by my failure to make contact that I didn't know what to say or how to act. He makes me . . . nervous. I can't think clearly when I'm around him. I probably ruined the whole experiment."

"Jay showed up here? At the lab?"

Susannah nodded abjectly.

"Did he explain what brought him here?"

"No. In fact, he wanted to know that same thing himself. He claimed he saw me following him around campus. I don't see how he could have. I was very discreet."

"How close did you get to him?"

Susannah shrugged. "I don't know. Not close enough, obviously. The first time at the water fountain, maybe four or five feet. Outside Parker Hall, maybe ten feet at best."

"And you're sure he didn't see you?"

"Maybe he did. I suppose he could have. Why else would he accuse me of following him?"

"And how were you dressed?"

"The same way I was when I left, except for the big mud stain on the front of my coat, a pair of waterlogged shoes, torn panty hose and a scraped knee. I looked like Miss America," she added sarcastically.

"And you were wearing the potion?"

"Of course. That was the whole point."

"Exactly. That was the whole point." Lauren looked at Susannah expectantly.

"What?" Susannah said impatiently.

"Earth to Dr. Hart, Earth to Dr. Hart. Susannah, it works! The potion works! That's why Jay Beaumont turned up here this afternoon."

Susannah looked at her assistant, shocked out of her glum mood. She opened her mouth to refute Lauren's claim, but then snapped it shut without saying a word. Could Lauren be right? Could the potion have brought Jay to her lab?

"Susannah, I've tested the potion over distance and the pheromone is detectable up to ten feet away on a calm day, even farther if you're upwind."

"At the Student Union, I was standing upwind," Susannah said. "And outside Parker Hall I was, too. I remember because my hair kept blowing in my eyes."

"It works!" Lauren jumped up and down, then pulled Susannah from the stool and did a little jig. "It works, it works, it works! And you didn't even have to make contact. The potion did it all."

Susannah quickly backtracked through their encounter, evaluating it objectively. Lauren was right. It was as if Jay Beaumont had been drawn to her lab by an outside force, something beyond his control. His actions and his words pointed directly to the potion. A smile broke across Susannah's face. How could she have missed it? Her mind had been so muddled by his sudden and unexplained appearance at her lab that she'd nearly overlooked the most important breakthrough of her scientific career.

All the possibilities of the potion raced through her mind. Couples in deteriorating relationships could be given the potion to prevent a breakup and restore the initial intensity of their feelings for each other. Infidelity would be wiped out in the twenty-first century, much like polio and smallpox had been in centuries before. And with premarital DNA screening, couples could be warned of impending trouble and incompatibility. Given the proper manufacturing and marketing, the cost to the consumer could be kept in the affordable range, making Susannah's potion available to people of all walks of life. Her dreams were on the verge of coming true.

Lauren suddenly stopped her dance and dragged Susannah over to a pair of stools. "All right, out with it. What happened after the besotted Mr. Beaumont showed up here?"

Susannah hesitated, wondering how much she should tell Lauren, then decided to be honest. "I was leaving the lab to go to the supply room and I opened the door and there he was. First he said—"

"Cut to the chase," Lauren interrupted. "Give me specific sexual behaviors."

Susannah drew a deep breath. "He kissed me."

Lauren's eyes widened. "Really? How does he kiss?"

"He placed his lips on mine and then...well, you know what happens. It's common behavior among primates. Baboons do it all the time. So do chimps."

"I strongly doubt that Jay Beaumont kisses like a chimp! How did it feel?"

Susannah paused, trying to come up with the appropriate dispassionate description. But discussing Jay Beaumont's technique without passion was like discussing Einstein without mentioning the word genius. Jay Beaumont was definitely MENSA material when it came to kissing. "It felt . . . Well, there was . . . firm pressure on the lips. Some activity from the tongue. That felt wet and warm. And he didn't confine his kisses to the mouth. He moved to the neck, also."

"And how did his kisses make *you* feel?"

"I felt . . ." Incredible, Susannah wanted to say. Jittery and warm and breathless all at once. As though she wanted him to go on and— "It doesn't matter how his kisses made me feel," she said. "*I'm* not the subject of the experiment. Mr. Beaumont is."

"Now that we have proof that the potion works on humans, we can finally publicize our findings!" Lauren said excitedly.

"Hold on. Not yet. We know the potion works as a primary attractant, but now we need to study its long-term effectiveness. We need to see how long Jay remains attracted, *without* reciprocal female interest."

Lauren gave her a dubious look. "Jay looks like he might be a hard man to resist."

"I'm a scientist," Susannah answered, attempting to inject a note of conviction into her voice. "I'm trained to maintain my objectivity. But I do think it would be a good idea to organize our data and start preparing our report. And with Derwin lurking in the shadows, it might be best to take everything home and work on it there." Susannah considered telling Lauren about Derwin's strange behavior, but knowing Lauren's distaste for the guy, she decided to keep it to herself. She would deal with Derwin on her own.

"What's next?" Lauren asked. "When do you see Beaumont again?"

"We've made a dinner date," Susannah replied.

"Ah, the obligatory dinner date. A common courtship ritual, where the male offers food in exchange for sex," Lauren teased. "Even male roadrunners bring the female roadrunner a lizard or two to smooth the way."

Susannah shot her assistant an anxious smile. "Well, I don't care if he shows up at my door with a herd of lizards, there's no way Jay Beaumont is going to trade food for sex with me!"

THE PILE OF CLOTHING on Susannah's bed was growing larger by the minute. She held a deep-green silk shirt-waist dress in front of her, then tossed it on the top of the heap. Everything in her closet, with the exception of Lauren's red dress, was painfully plain—exactly the kind of clothing she should want to wear on a dinner date with Jay Beaumont. So why was she so tempted to throw aside her conservative wardrobe and put on the silly sequined thing?

Hesitantly she reached into her closet and pulled out the glittering dress. Maybe she was simply curious. Though wearing the dress had made her uncomfortable, when Jay had turned his eyes on her she had felt an incredible sense of feminine power. What could a woman do with that power? What could she make Jay Beaumont do?

Susannah closed her eyes and sighed. First the red dress and now the potion. She couldn't help but wonder what it would feel like to have Jay look at the real Susannah Hart the way he had looked at Desirée. Or to kiss the real Susannah Hart the way he had kissed a scientist steeped in a powerful pheromone.

She tossed the dress on the pile with the others. Why think about something that would never be? Without the potion, Jay Beaumont would never have given Susannah a second look. She had accepted her lack of sex appeal long ago. And her introverted nature assured her that Desirée and her sexy ways would stay dead and buried.

Susannah glanced at the bedside clock. Jay was due to pick her up in ten minutes, and like some lovesick schoolgirl, she was worrying about what to wear! She yanked a simple black dress from the back of her closet and pulled it on, then hurried to the bathroom to fix her hair.

When the doorbell rang ten minutes later, Susannah was waiting nervously on the couch, the black dress hidden beneath her gray wool coat, her hair pulled back in an inconspicuous knot at her nape. The potion was still damp on her wrists and neck. With a stab of apprehension, she rose and answered the door.

A tiny bouquet of violets greeted her, and behind them the handsome face of Jay Beaumont. *In addition to food, the male will often present small gifts—jewelry, clothing, flowers—as an enticement for an intimate liaison.* Susannah stifled a moan as Dr. Gruber's words drifted through her mind. Though she had tried to convince herself she was ready for this date, she hadn't really realized what she would be up against until this moment. Jay had an obvious appetite for seduction; their encounter in the lab had proved that. Now, with another dose of the potion thrown into the mix, she feared she was about to become the evening's main course.

Rather than allow Jay into the privacy of her home, she took the flowers and pulled the front door shut behind her. "Thank you. They're very nice," she said, avoiding his gaze.

He took her elbow as they walked down the steps from the porch. "You're welcome," he replied. "I saw them and I thought of you."

She glanced up and caught him smiling. Pretty words, but he had probably said them a hundred times to a hundred different women, using a variety of floral arrangements. "And why would violets make you think of me?" she inquired warily.

He pulled open the door to his car and helped her in. "I don't know. Maybe because at first glance they seem

like such an innocent flower. But when one inhales their
scent, they suddenly become something more...exotic."

His words sent shivers down her spine and she swallowed convulsively. How close he had come to the truth!
Susannah stole a glance at him, wondering if he knew
something, but he smiled innocently, then pulled away
and slammed the car door.

She looked down at the violets, then up at Jay as he
crossed in front of the car. If the man could turn a simple
bouquet of violets into a thinly disguised sexual propo-
sition, what would he do with a five-course meal? Realizing she wasn't prepared to find out, she reached for
the door handle, ready to run back into her house and
lock the door behind her.

But determination got the better of her. She wouldn't
make a mess of this opportunity. Jay Beaumont was a
gentleman. If things went too far, she would call upon
his inbred chivalry and tell him to stop. And if that didn't
work, a swift slap on the face or a well-placed kick to the
groin would. She would be the one to control the events
of the evening.

Jay slipped into the driver's seat and started the car. He
glanced over his shoulder and the Jaguar leapt smoothly
from the curb into traffic. "I thought we'd take the sce-
nic route to the Canterbury," he said. "The ice is off the
lake and the trees haven't filled in yet, so we'll be able to
see the water nearly the whole way."

"The highway is much faster," Susannah replied. "And
isn't our reservation for seven-thirty? We wouldn't want
to be late."

He glanced over at her. "I called and told them we'd
be a little late. I have something I want to show you." He
fixed his attention back on the road and before long they
were winding their way around the north shore of Ge-

neva Lake. Jay had been right. The view was spectacu-
lar, the last rays of the setting sun glinting off the water.
He slowed as they came around a curve, then to her surprise turned into a narrow gravel driveway. The car de-
scended a steep hill until at last it reached lake level. Jay
put the car in park, then shut the engine off.

The view to the lake was unobstructed, but it was
nothing they couldn't have seen from the road. To the left
of the driveway was a ramshackle cabin, and to the right,
a huge dilapidated shed. Whatever Jay had brought her
here for, it certainly wasn't the view. Whispered words
from the girls at Emily Dickinson came to mind, words
like "parking" and "necking" and a strange reference to
"submarine races." What went on in the back seats of
cars on deserted roads was the stuff of schoolgirl gossip
and something that Susannah hadn't ever experienced.
And all these things went on *without* the aid of a powerful potion. A sense of foreboding overwhelmed her.

"We're stopping here?" she asked, her voice cracking
slightly.

Jay nodded, his gaze taking in the landscape.

"Are we . . . parking?"

He turned and gave her a bemused look, before he
opened the driver's side door. "We're parked," he said,
before he stepped out. He jogged around to her side and
opened the door. "And now we're going to walk."
Reaching in, he grabbed her hand and pulled her from
the car.

The ground was soft and Susannah had trouble keeping up with Jay as he strode toward the shed. When he
reached the door, he fished in his coat pockets, then
pulled out a key that unlocked a rusty padlock. The door
swung open on squeaky hinges and Susannah peered
into a dark, dank interior.

"There's a lantern inside," he said.

"What's in here?"

"Come in and find out."

Susannah stepped into the shed as a lantern sputtered to light. The golden glow cast shadows over a huge hulk, covered with a dusty tarp. "Is this what we're here to see?" she asked. So this wasn't part of a seduction scheme, she realized. He actually wanted to show her something. And from the looks of it, it wasn't going to be his etchings. His attention had suddenly been captivated by whatever was hidden beneath a piece of mildewed canvas. But her relief was tempered with confusion. Suddenly the potion seemed to have lost its effect on him.

Jay grinned and grabbed a corner of the tarp. Slowly, and with a great stirring of dust, he pulled it away. Then he stepped back to her side and crossed his arms in front of him, gazing proudly at a wooden sailboat. "It was designed and built in 1948 by a man from Virginia named Marcus Townsend. It's hull number one, the first he built. He handcrafted five of these boats before he died. He called them *Ospreys* after the fish hawks near his home. Only one of his *Ospreys* was known to survive, until yesterday. Until I found this one."

Her gaze ran along the immense scaffolding that held the boat up off the ground. "How did you find it?" she asked, drawn into his fascination with the dusty, old relic.

He walked up to the boat and ran his palm along the hull. "I was walking around near the marina last weekend and I got to talking with a man who runs a sail repair shop out of his garage. He told me about it. The boat hasn't been on the water in over thirty years."

"So you bought it?"

He laughed, never taking his eyes off the boat. "In a way. I bought the shed and the land under the shed. And the cabin. And the owner threw the boat in with the deal."

"You bought waterfront property on Geneva Lake just to get a boat?"

"I would have bought a million acres of useless swampland in Arizona for *this* boat," he said.

She moved to join him. "It's that special, then?"

He turned and nodded, giving her a satisfied smile. "Yeah," he said. "It's that special. Townsend was a naval architect. He designed warships for the U.S. Navy during the Second World War. And when the war was over, he resigned his commission and retired to design and build sailboats. He was a brilliant man, a man who hoped that elegant little sloops would be his legacy to sailing, rather than ships of war."

Susannah followed him as he walked around the sailboat. "I understand you're working on a book on naval engineering."

"Mmm-hmm," he answered distractedly. "Would you like to climb on board?"

The boyish excitement in his eyes was too much to resist and Susannah nodded. Jay dragged a ladder from the far wall and leaned it against the boat. Then, wrapped in the circle of his arms, she climbed the ladder with him until they reached the deck of the boat. Jay helped her into the cockpit and she sat down. He took a place across from her, leaning back and stretching his legs out in a relaxed manner.

After a long silence he spoke. "I learned to sail when I was eight years old. My dad owned a boatyard and we always had at least one sailboat. Have you ever been sailing?"

Susannah shook her head.

"It's the most powerful feeling—to be out on the water with only the wind to move your boat. It's peaceful, yet exciting. There's nothing like it. I can remember the adventures I used to have on the water with my brothers. Me and Jeff and Jack—back then we were inseparable." The warmth faded from his expression. "Then we grew up and things changed."

"What changed?" Susannah asked.

He shrugged. "We forgot how much we loved sailing. And each other, I guess. Things came between us that couldn't be repaired by a broad reach on the Bay." He paused. "You know, I built my first boat with my father when I was ten. We launched it on the Chesapeake on the Fourth of July. That's when I decided that I wanted to join the navy and build ships."

"Is your father still alive?"

"He and my mother still live in the house I grew up in. My dad works part-time at the Beaumont Boatyards building twenty-five-foot daysailers like this one. But now Beaumont Boatyards builds custom yachts for millionaire clients. It's just a tiny part of Beaumont Industries, but it's the best part."

Once again they fell into a companionable silence. Susannah had thought she'd known Jay Beaumont, but the man sitting across from her was nothing like the man who teased and tormented her dreams, the man who had set her research on end. He'd dropped his smooth, practiced charm and was now as open and approachable as an old friend. For the first time since she'd met him, she felt relaxed in his presence.

"Tell me about your work," he said. "Mitch says you know everything there is to know about mud turtles."

She couldn't help but smile. "A rather dubious claim to fame," she replied. "I'm really studying how environmental changes are impacting the reproduction cycles of reptiles."

"And when you're not watching turtles doing it, what do you do for fun?"

Susannah paused, then frowned. "I watch more turtles...doing it, I guess. My work is fun. It's what I like to do."

"The mark of a true voyeur," he teased. Jay stood and pulled her up in front of him, running his hands along her arms. "I can see we're going to have to introduce you to more stimulating recreational pursuits," he said softly.

Susannah stiffened as the old Jay Beaumont reappeared, complete with sexy innuendos and devastating charm. "I—I think we'd better get going," she said. "We'll be late for our dinner reservation."

The grin faded from his face to be replaced by a tight smile. "Sure. Let's go."

Jay helped her back down the ladder, then locked the shed behind them before they headed toward the car. He suddenly seemed remote and aloof, and she wondered if she had said something wrong. She stopped beside the car and waited for him to open the door for her. When he didn't, she turned around to find him staring at her, an oddly enigmatic expression on his face.

Slowly he reached out to run his fingers across her cheek. She instinctively turned her face to his hand, wanting more of his touch, but he pulled it away.

"You had a smudge on your cheek," he murmured. "That shed is dirty."

Mesmerized, Susannah reached out and brushed her thumb along his jaw, wiping away a grimy streak. "I'm not the only one with a dirty face," she said, holding up her fingers as evidence. "The Canterbury requires a jacket and tie, but I don't think dust and grime are part of the dress code."

He smiled, then moved closer. They stood motionless for a long time, Susannah's back pressed against the car, Jay's arm braced beside her head and his mouth hovering over hers. The air seemed to hum around them with the intensity of unspoken desire. Susannah's earlier doubts about the potion disappeared, along with her resolve to keep Jay Beaumont at a safe distance.

She swallowed hard, then attempted to speak. "Will it float?" she croaked.

"Will what float?" he murmured, his breath warm against her lips.

"The boat. Will the boat float?"

He drew away, a puzzled look on his face. "Yeah, it'll float. It's old, but it's only been sailed in fresh water. I've got some work to do on it, but I hope to put it in in a few weeks."

Susannah ran her hand along the car door until she found the handle, then turned and pulled the door open. "Good," she replied. "I think we'd better be going."

The twenty-minute drive to the Canterbury Inn was passed in near silence, Jay making an occasional inane comment about the scenery and Susannah acknowledging the comment with a few stilted words. Her attention was drawn to the side-view mirror and she distractedly watched a car that had followed them since they'd left the driveway of Jay's property. She was surprised when the car pulled in behind them, but pushed the coincidence out of her mind as she and Jay walked up the front steps of the huge Victorian inn.

The Canterbury was an old summer house, built around the turn of the century by a wealthy Chicago industrialist and recently restored and converted to a bed-and-breakfast. The white clapboard structure sat on a stunning piece of lakefront property, with a wide sweeping lawn that led to a long, lit pier. It brought forth visions of the Great Gatsby and Susannah was surprised to find herself entranced by the romantic setting.

They paused on the wide veranda to brush the dust from their clothes, then Jay pulled the front door open and they entered. A hostess took their coats and immediately showed them to a table. Jay ordered a bottle of wine and while they waited, they listened to the soft strains of a jazz ballad being played on a piano in the corner of the dining room.

"Would you like to dance?" Jay asked.

"No one's dancing," she replied. The words were barely out of her mouth before she realized that they had played this scene before. A small measure of irritation surfaced at the thought that she was just one of many who had been charmed into dancing with Jay Beaumont on an empty dance floor.

"Then we'd have the entire dance floor to ourselves, wouldn't we?" he said with inscrutable aplomb.

How she wanted to say yes, to slip into his arms and move around the dance floor, his body pressed against hers. *Resistance*, her mind warned. She had already given in to his charm once and the evening wasn't even half over.

"I can't dance," Susannah said flatly.

"Of course you—" He stopped suddenly, then reached out and grabbed his wineglass. "Of course, if you don't want to, we don't have to."

A waiter appeared and took their orders, and the conversation turned to the university. They talked about exasperating students and hectic class schedules and annoying colleagues. Not once, to Susannah's relief, did they venture into more personal territory. But again, she was confused at the strangely intermittent effects of the potion. As soon as the waiter cleared their main course, she excused herself to find the ladies' room and dab more of the pheromone on her pulse points.

As she walked through the dining room, a soft voice called her name. Susannah spun around and watched as a lone diner lowered a wine menu to reveal a startlingly familiar face.

"Derwin! What are you doing here?" Susannah whispered.

"I've come to keep you from making a terrible mistake," Derwin said.

"What are you talking about?" Susannah glanced around to see if their conversation had been noticed. She looked over at Jay, but his back was partially turned as he gazed out the wide front window at the lake. Susannah stalked to the entrance, then motioned to Derwin to follow her. "Come on," she ordered.

Like a recalcitrant child, Derwin stood and exited the dining room a few seconds behind her. Susannah's mind raced as she nervously paced the length of the inn's elegant foyer. What was Derwin doing here? Had he purposely followed them? She remembered the car that had driven into the parking lot right behind them. He *had* followed them! But why? Was he on another spying mission for Dr. Curtis? Did he know about her experiment?

"Explain yourself, Mr. Erwin. Why are you here?"

"I—I'm having dinner," he stammered.

"Alone? At a romantic country inn? I find that hard to believe. Did Dr. Curtis send you?"

"Dr. Curtis?" Perplexed, Derwin shook his head. "No, I came on my own. You look lovely tonight, Susannah."

Ignoring his compliment, she walked back to the entrance to the dining room and peeked in. Jay was still staring out the window.

"You followed me here, didn't you?"

Derwin nodded enthusiastically. "I almost lost you a few times. And when you stopped at the lake, I wasn't sure—"

"You were there? At the lake?"

"Yes. I was hiding in the bushes," he said in a serious, reprimanding tone. "He's no good for you, Susannah. It's not safe to wander around in the woods with a man of his character."

With another frantic peek into the dining room, Susannah could see that Jay was getting restless. "Who I choose to associate with is my own business. I want you to leave. Now," Susannah ordered, a note of desperation in her voice. "We'll discuss your concerns on Monday."

"I'd be happy to drive you home, Susannah. I noticed you were finished with dinner and—"

"Mr. Erwin! If you don't go, I'll put in a call to Dr. Curtis and we'll settle this thing tonight."

Derwin hung his head and pouted like a petulant child. "All right. I'll leave. But I have to pay for my dinner first."

"I'll pay for your dinner," Susannah said. "Just go— now!"

He slowly walked to the front door, casting a dejected look in her direction. When the door closed behind him, Susannah breathed a deep sigh of relief. Opening her purse, she drew out a vial of the potion and quickly dabbed a generous amount on her neck and wrists, then hurriedly paid the hostess for Derwin's dinner before rushing back into the dining room.

Jay stood as she approached the table, and pulled out her chair for her. "I was wondering where you were. I was beginning to think that you'd ditched me," he joked.

Susannah smiled haltingly as she settled into her chair. "Have you been ditched often?"

"Only by you," he replied in a teasing voice.

And Desirée, she thought. "Well, then, I wouldn't want to do any more damage to your fragile ego. Besides, I'm having a lovely time," Susannah said in an attempt to reassure him. She paused. "Would it be all right if we left now?" Though she had ordered Derwin off the premises, she wasn't sure he'd obey. If he and Jay met again, there would be some serious explanations required. And she wasn't sure she'd be able to provide them. Whatever was going on in Derwin's head, she was certain that it had something to do with her potion research. She just wasn't sure what.

"You don't want dessert or coffee?"

"No, the meal was quite filling. I don't think I could eat another bite."

Jay motioned for the check and moments later they were standing on the front porch. Susannah searched the shrubbery for any sign of Derwin. If he was there, he was well hidden.

"Would you like to walk out to the end of the pier?" Jay asked.

Lined with golden lights, the whitewashed pier beckoned to her and Susannah nodded. With Derwin gone, there was no need to end their evening immediately. "That would be nice."

Though the air was crisp, the weather had warmed considerably during the past few days and spring was definitely upon them. Their footsteps echoed hollowly against the planks of the pier. When they reached the end of the T-shaped dock, they turned left and sat down on a bench facing the lake at the far end. The gentle lap of the water against the pier relaxed Susannah. She took in a deep breath and exhaled slowly.

She felt Jay's arm on the back of the bench and she leaned into it as it encircled her shoulders. They sat in silence, watching the twinkling lights of downtown Lake Geneva across the water.

"Do you ever wonder what it is that brings two people together?" Jay asked in a soft voice.

Susannah's heart flopped in her chest. Jay Beaumont had developed a habit of asking the most disconcerting questions. "What do you mean?"

He shrugged and continued to stare out at the water. "Like you and me. We could have gone forever without meeting each other. The campus is large and I'm only here for a semester. Yet through a strange series of events, we met. And now we're sitting here. Is it fate? Or random chance?"

Susannah turned to him and studied his expression. What was he getting at? She felt as if he were toying with her in some way, as if he knew something more than she had allowed. "I don't believe in fate," she replied warily. "What do you think?"

He turned to her and stared down into her eyes, the soft light casting his features in angles and planes. "I think..." He paused. "I think..." He gently cupped her chin in his palm. "I think I'd like to kiss you again."

"You would?" she breathed.

"Very much," he replied. "May I?"

Susannah nodded slowly, her gaze captured by his, all her resolve scattered like dust in the wind. Why couldn't she resist him? With achingly deliberate movements, he reached back and began to remove the hairpins that held her hair tightly bound at her nape. One by one they dropped with a soft clink onto the pier, like music in the silence of the cold night air. When he had removed the last one, he ran his fingers through the knot, spreading her hair across her shoulders and back.

"There," he murmured. "That's better."

His hands moved back to her face and he gently traced the line of her jaw with his thumbs. His mouth found hers and suddenly she was lost in a mind-numbing kiss. His tongue danced magically over her lips and she responded, opening her mouth to receive his gentle invasion. The kiss deepened, until she was driven mindless with desire, grasping at the lapels of his topcoat and pulling him closer still.

Slowly reality seeped into her consciousness, urging her to stop and consider what she was doing. At first she tried to brush the nagging appeal for restraint away, but try as she might, the guilt returned. She was in the midst of a terrible breach in scientific propriety. With a soft moan, she pulled back, pushing gently against his chest with her hands. "I—I think we'd better go."

Jay took a deep breath and held it for a long moment, before exhaling in a cloud of vapor. He reluctantly stood and took her hand. As they strolled back to the main pier, Susannah kept her eyes down. But a distant rustle of bushes caught her attention and she looked up to see a tall dark form appearing from the shrubbery. The clumsy gait was more than familiar and she held her breath as Derwin casually passed them on the lawn, his head down, his face hidden in shadow.

She glanced over at Jay, only to find his attention focused on the bright lights of the inn. Then she looked over her shoulder. Derwin had turned to watch them, walking backward as he stared in her direction. She shot him a narrow-eyed glare. He was coming perilously close to the edge of a large clump of barberry bushes and she quickly turned away and picked up her pace.

They were halfway up the lawn when it happened. The sound of breaking branches and the subsequent yelp were loud enough to be heard in the main dining room. Jay spun around at the noise and squinted into the darkness. "What was that?" he asked.

Susannah tugged at his arm. "Probably some animal. A skunk or maybe a weasel."

"No, wait. I think someone's out there. Yeah! There he is."

Her eyes followed his direction and she saw Derwin in a spill of light from the pier, struggling through the bushes on his hands and knees.

"I'd better go help him," Jay said.

"He looks like he's fine," Susannah insisted. "He's probably embarrassed enough as it is. See? There, he's already made it out."

Jay watched for a moment more before he reluctantly resumed their walk. "I wonder what he's doing out here alone? He probably had a little too much wine with dinner. Or maybe he lost something."

"His mind, if I don't miss my guess," Susannah mumbled to herself.

As JAY WATCHED Susannah run up her front sidewalk and into her house, he felt like driving right back to Geneva Lake and taking a cold midnight swim. With a hiss of frustration, he stalked back to his car and jumped in.

What had he done wrong? All the signs were there. He was certain that she wanted him to kiss her again. And it wasn't as if she were repulsed by the way he kissed— her behavior on the dock disproved that theory. But, with a quick smile and a nervous "Good night," she had firmly stopped him from taking what seemed natural. His fantasies of dragging her into her bedroom and discovering the pleasures hidden deep inside the mysterious Dr. Hart disappeared in a puff of smoke. And once again, he was treated to the sight of her backside as she hurried away from him.

Maybe it was the mystery surrounding Dr. Hart that intrigued him. He knew she was hiding something, but what was it? Had someone hurt her so deeply in the past that she was afraid to get involved with another man? Or was inexperience keeping her away? Maybe she was frightened of him . . . or his reputation. He had heard the stories floating around campus and until now had found them vastly amusing.

Damn! He had never met a woman who ran as hot and cold as Susannah Hart!

But, then, he'd never met a woman like Susannah at all. He'd always found himself attracted to sophisticated, self-assured women whose beauty ran no deeper than their flawless faces and perfectly toned bodies. An image of Cynthia came to mind, but he brushed it away in irritation. Such a cunning manipulator hidden behind a beautiful facade. How had he been so blind, so gullible? Everyone loved Cynthia, yet the only person *she* ever truly loved was herself.

He now realized that since the breakup of his marriage, he'd unknowingly been on an endless quest for the perfect woman. And now he'd finally found her. But she wasn't exactly what he'd expected. Her beauty ran deep, beyond the surface, into her very soul. When she smiled, he lost himself in the warmth, and when she frowned, he felt desperate to wipe away her troubles. With no more than cursory encouragement, he found himself captivated by her guileless radiance.

Most times she seemed almost innocent, as if she lacked any real experience in the ways of desire, as if she were unaware of her effect on him. But then her naive facade would shift a bit and he would glimpse a sexy wanton in her place. Dr. Hart or Desirée? He couldn't seem to separate the two. But who was the *real* Susannah?

More and more, he was beginning to believe that even she didn't know. Though Mitch's research story was worth considering, Jay was nearly certain that Susannah's behavior had nothing to do with scientific research. He sensed that if she was doing research, it was something of a more personal nature. She was testing the waters, taking a walk on the wild side, finding out what she was missing cooped up in her safe, little laboratory.

He had thought to let her discover her sensual side in her own good time. But no matter how much determination she seemed to muster, she still couldn't take that next step. The step that would lead her into his arms and into his bed. And he was getting impatient.

Jay started the Jag, then pulled away from the curb. He glanced at the clock on the dash. Ten-thirty. He couldn't remember the last time a dinner date had ended so early. Or the last time he'd truly wanted a dinner date to go on until dawn, as he did now. He flipped on the radio and tuned in a Chicago jazz station. Then he picked up his car phone and dialed Mitch's number. A cold beer in a noisy bar filled with attentive women was just what he needed right now. Mitch's phone rang ten times before Jay finally hung up.

He'd be spending the evening alone, a far cry from what he had anticipated when the evening had begun.

But somehow, it didn't bother him. There would be other opportunities to expand Susannah Hart's horizons. He would just have to be patient and wait until she was ready. He was certain it would be worth the wait.

6

SUSANNAH LOOKED OUT across the wide sea of faces. Her lecture hall was filled today, as it had been for the past three sessions. That all her students were in attendance was no mean feat—this was Anthropology 101, a course she had been forced to teach when the regular professor had fallen ill and Dr. Curtis had learned of her undergraduate major. It was springtime, the sun was shining and students were more inclined to spend their late mornings sunbathing. But the fact that most of her students had brought their friends to class only proved that even education, when packaged with a little sex, could be sold to the public.

During the past three weeks, Susannah had been covering the sexual habits of animals and relating them to the sexual behaviors of humans, a subject that had drawn an unusually high number of temporary auditors. Susannah glanced at the clock. She had four more pages of lecture notes to fit into five more minutes of class.

"I'd like to return to our examination of the pygmy chimps, commonly referred to as bonobos, a species that can be observed in the swampy areas along the Congo. In the bonobos we find many behavior patterns that we find in humans." Susannah put an overhead on the projector and went through the list.

"With the bonobos, we see sex used not only as a means of procreation but as a means of daily recreation, as a way to reduce stress."

"All right!" a voice called from the audience.

Susannah glared in the direction of the shout, then continued.

"Kissing is a prevalent bonobo behavior used as a prelude to the sex act. Like humans, bonobos participate in what we have come to call French kissing." A few titters of amusement sounded from the lecture hall. "I'm sure I don't need to explain the terminology here," she added.

"Charles Darwin postulated that kissing is a natural behavior in humans, and in fact over ninety percent of humans kiss. In some African cultures, though, kissing is unknown, and some societies find the practice disgusting."

"They've never kissed *me!*" another voice called.

Susannah contained a smile. Toward the end of these classes, the students usually liked to lighten up the atmosphere with a few ribald comments. "If they had, I'm sure they would find you just as disgusting," she replied. The lecture hall broke into a round of enthusiastic applause.

"Though bonobos come the closest to human sexual behavior in the primate kingdom, they do exhibit some marked differences. Bonobos are not monogamous, they do not form long-term pairs, nor do they raise offspring in pairs. To anthropologists, the bonobo's promiscuity is living proof that adultery is a human trait that can be traced back to the beginnings of the human race.

"This concludes our discussion on sexual behaviors. I'd like to thank all of our auditing students for coming and I invite you to take the test along with our registered students next Thursday. For next time, read chapters twelve and thirteen and be prepared to discuss them in this week's small-group sessions."

The room gradually cleared while Susannah gathered her lecture notes and books. When she looked up, she noticed a figure standing at the back of the hall in the shadows of the balcony. She watched as Jay moved into the light and down the aisle toward the podium. She lost herself in the easy grace of his stride. He was dressed casually in well-worn jeans and a bright-teal rugby shirt. His rugged leather jacket gave him an almost dangerous air. He looked—

Suddenly her heart stopped as she realized she was not wearing the potion. Furtively she glanced over at her purse, but there was no way to get to the vial without Jay noticing.

"You're quite popular with the students," he commented as he approached.

"It's the subject matter, not the teacher," she replied with a nervous smile. "How long have you been here?"

He stood with the podium between them and crossed his arms on the front edge. "I came in during the discourse on gorilla harems. Imagine that! Females who reject monogamy and seek out the pleasures found in a harem. When did we humans make a wrong turn?"

She busied herself with straightening her lecture notes. "Around three and a half million years ago by my calculations," Susannah answered. "Males of the species have always gravitated toward polygamy, but many females find pair-bonding to be desirable."

"Tell that to my ex-wife," Jay muttered.

Susannah looked at him, shocked. "I didn't realize you'd been married."

"I try not to think about it," Jay replied. "It was a long time ago."

"What happened?"

"Is this scientific or personal curiosity, Dr. Hart?" Jay asked.

"Purely scientific," she answered. She knew she was lying before the words had left her lips. She had spent more than enough time trying to get to know Jay Beaumont scientifically. Maybe it was time to find out a little more about what made the man tick. Somehow she had never imagined Jay Beaumont in a monogamous relationship. He acted as if he had been born to bachelorhood.

"She had an affair with my brother," he said bluntly.

"I'm sorry," Susannah replied, her voice soft and sympathetic. She could tell that the scars ran deep. It was hard to imagine any woman giving up a man like Jay. Even at his worst, he was still irresistible. "You know, in some societies, adultery is an accepted practice. In many Inuit cultures, it's deemed an honor to offer one's wife to a friend or business associate. And in medieval Scotland, with a custom known as *jus primae noctis*, a vassal offered his bride to his feudal lord on their wedding night."

His jaw tensed and she could sense his carefully controlled anger. Providing a rationalization for his wife's infidelity was not having a positive effect on his suddenly sullen mood. She was tempted to reach out and brush the lines of tension from his face, but she quelled the impulse. It was not her place to initiate any sexual contact.

"But, then, monogamy has a long and illustrious list of supporters. The toad, the dung beetle and desert wood lice are all monogamous." That bit of trivia brought a crooked smile to his lips and she felt a glimmer of satisfaction run through her as his handsome face lost its icy mask. "And some animals, like the dwarf mongoose and the dik-dik, mate for life. Though, with the exception of the human race, monogamy is rare in mammals."

"And why is that?" Jay asked as he grabbed the stack of books from her arms and guided her down the steps to the aisle. His fingers grasped her elbow and she found her attention focused there, on the warmth and the tingle it sent shooting through her limb.

"It's not to the male's benefit," she answered distract-. edly. "He can pass on more of his genes if he has a number of mates. And as for females, a single male is much more trouble than he's worth. Many female mammals prefer to live with female relatives and copulate with—" Susannah came to a dead stop in the middle of the aisle, a warm blush creeping up her cheeks. She was so used to speaking frankly about sex that sometimes she slipped into "professor speak" at the most inappropriate times.

"With?" Jay prompted.

"With visitors," she said uncomfortably. "So, you see, nature gives us a long precedent for philandering and a weak case for devotion."

"But nature, Mrs. Allnut, is what we are put into this world to rise above," Jay quipped.

Susannah frowned. "What? Who's Mrs. Allnut?"

"It's actually supposed to be *Mr.* Allnut," Jay explained.

Susannah searched her mind for the name, wondering if Allnut was some obscure anthropologist. "I still don't—"

"*African Queen*? Katharine Hepburn and Humphrey Bogart?"

Susannah shook her head.

"You've never seen *The African Queen*?"

"I assume you're talking about a movie?"

"Not just a movie, a classic! You'd love it. It's a terrific story about an adventurous boat captain and an uptight missionary and a trip they take down the Nile."

"I don't have much time for popular culture," Susannah replied.

"You need to make time for this. One of the student film societies is holding a Bogart festival next week. They're showing *The African Queen* on Tuesday. Would you like to go?"

"You're asking me out? On a date?" Susannah was dumbfounded. How could this be? She wasn't wearing the potion! She scrambled for an explanation. Could the potion possibly have a carryover effect, one that lasted beyond actual direct exposure? The question fascinated her and she immediately decided to test the theory. Just how long would Jay's interest be sustained without another application of the potion?

Jay put his arm around her shoulders. "Yes, I'm asking you out on a date. We had a great time at the Canterbury. Why shouldn't we go out again?"

"No reason," she murmured. "I'd love to see *The Amazon Queen* with you."

"I BELIEVE she did the right thing by leaving him," Susannah said firmly.

She stopped on the sidewalk in front of her house and turned to Jay. He held tight to her hand as he had during the entire walk home from the Bogart Film Festival on campus. They had just seen *Casablanca*, their fourth Bogart film in as many nights. He grabbed her other hand and smiled warmly.

"How can you say that?" he teased. "He's Bogart. She belonged with him."

Susannah shook her head. "But it goes against all the rules of permanent pair-bonding. Women choose men who can provide for them, men who are loyal, men who will stick around and protect them. Mr. Blaine was a womanizer and a rogue. Mr. Laszlo was brave and honorable. Ilse made the proper choice."

Jay laughed. "Ah, my ever-practical Susannah. You have such a unique way of looking at things." He reached out and smoothed back a hair from her face. His expression turned serious. "Maybe that's why I like being with you so much."

A tiny shiver ran through her at his touch. She glanced away toward the direction of the front door, then looked back at him and smiled hesitantly. "I—I'd better go in."

He bent over and brushed his lips against hers in a fleeting kiss. Sudden longing raced through her and she fought the urge to throw her arms around his neck and bring back the passion they had shared in their early encounters, those deep, soul-shattering embraces that had plagued her fantasies from dawn until dusk. Lately she had had to satisfy herself with his very chaste and non-demanding kisses and his reserved, polite manner.

How much longer could this possibly go on? She hadn't worn the potion in more than a week, yet his attraction was still viable. Though his predatory nature had been subdued, she knew he still wanted her. But she could tell his interest was definitely waning, and his kisses served as evidence. They were so . . . proper and well controlled.

"Can I come in?" he murmured.

Susannah hesitated. He had asked the same question every night this week and she had gently turned him down. But tonight was different. It was time to take an aggressive approach to her research, time to toss away her insecurities and fears and test the true extent of his desire. The potion's residual effect had been much stronger than she could have ever predicted. But just how strong was it?

"All right," she said, acquiescing. "Maybe for a little while." As soon as the invitation was out of her mouth, she regretted her decision. Was she really inviting him in to further her research? Or was she hoping to ignite his desire to its earlier intensity? Over the past week, she had felt her scientific objectivity grow cloudier with every encounter.

It was easy to resist Jay Beaumont when he assumed the role of glib bachelor. But he had changed during the course of the experiment and she was certain she was seeing the real man beneath the smooth, practiced facade. He was sweet and funny, nothing like the man she'd met while playing the sultry Desirée. He made her feel special, as if her plain looks and shyness made no difference to him at all, as if he saw past the clumsy, introverted Susannah to the woman that she really was.

She unlocked the front door and he followed her into her living room. "Can I take your jacket?" she said, twisting her hands in front of her.

Jay handed it to her, then flopped down on the couch and stretched his arm across the back. Her eyes were drawn to his chest, where the fabric of his pale-green polo shirt pulled taut over hard muscle. Worn jeans hugged his narrow hips and long legs. Whether he wore a business suit or dressed casually, there was no hiding the lean, athletic body beneath. She slipped out of her coat and threw both garments over a Stickley chair in the corner, then turned back to Jay with a forced smile.

"Can I get you anything to drink?"

"What do you have?"

Susannah cursed the fact that she'd asked. Beer would have been appropriate, but she hadn't expected to invite him in. "Water? Orange juice? I could make some coffee."

He shook his head, then patted the cushion beside him. "Forget the drinks. Why don't you sit down and relax."

"I—I think I'll have something to drink," she said, before rushing to the kitchen. She waited as long as she could in the kitchen, gathering her courage, then returned with a tall glass. Guardedly she sat down beside him on the edge of the couch and sipped the water.

Jay's attention wandered around the room and she watched him take in the stark mission-style furniture and the bare walls.

"This house suits you," he said.

"Because it's plain?"

He frowned. "No, not at all. It's very simple and functional. Everything in the room has a purpose. There's a strength to its simplicity."

She took another gulp of water, then shrugged. "I'm not much of a decorator. I don't like a lot of clutter." She jumped up from the couch and walked to the mantel to retrieve a small porcelain figurine of a hummingbird, then held it out to him. "Trochilidae. Lauren, my lab assistant, gave me this for Christmas last year. I would never have thought to buy it for myself, but I find that I enjoy looking at it. Even though it's just for decoration, I get pleasure from it." She put the bird back on the mantel and stroked the intricately painted feathers, her back to him. "You must find me terribly boring," she said.

A moment later, he was beside her at the fireplace. He took her by the shoulders and slowly turned her to face him. His gaze caught hers and he stared deeply into her eyes. "I find you endlessly fascinating," he replied.

"Why is that?"

"I've known a lot of women," he said, his statement matter-of-fact, "and I've found, when you scratch away the paint on the surface, many times the color doesn't go all the way through. But you're different. There's a . . . I don't know what to call it . . . a *realness* about you that goes deeper than the surface. I want to know the woman inside you, Susannah."

"The woman on the inside isn't much different from the woman on the outside," she replied.

"I don't believe that. I think there's more to you than meets the eye."

Susannah drew a shaky breath, then stepped out of his grasp. "Are you sure you wouldn't like something to drink?"

He frowned. "Why are you frightened of me, Susannah?"

She walked across the room, out of his reach and away from his keen gaze. "I— Well— " She swallowed convulsively as she studied her shoes. "I don't know what you want me to say." Why was this so difficult for her? She felt as if she were walking through broken glass, tiptoeing carefully, balancing and weaving, all the time fearful of that one false step. Why couldn't he see who she truly was? Why was he attaching some sort of silly feminine mystique to her?

The potion, she thought to herself. He wasn't beguiled by her; he was drawn to an image he had falsely associated with her. All the pain and disappointment of a lonely childhood came back to her in a rush. Would anyone ever love her for being just plain old Susannah Hart?

"There have been times when I wished I could be someone else," she began. "Someone prettier, more confident around others. But I can't change who I am, so I've learned to accept myself."

Jay stalked across the room and grabbed her shoulders again, this time more roughly. "Who told you you weren't pretty?"

"No one had to tell me," she said with a dry smile. "You forget, I'm intelligent and observant. I see the kind of women men are attracted to. I read the research."

Jay shook his head. "For a brilliant woman, sometimes you can be incredibly dumb, Dr. Hart." With that, his arm swept around her waist and he yanked her against his body. "Say it, Susannah," he murmured.

"Say what?" she said in a breathless voice.

"Say 'I am a beautiful woman.'"

She shook her head and attempted to twist away from him.

"Say it," he ordered.

"You are a beautiful woman," she said defiantly.

"Don't make a joke of this," he growled. "Say it."

"I—I can't."

"You can," he countered. His eyes, hard and unyielding, were fixed on her face and she felt the heat from his gaze burning her cheeks.

"I—I am a—a beautiful woman," she said.

His smile was devastating. "Yes, you are."

Slowly he lowered his head and his lips met hers. But this time the kiss was far from chaste. It was hot and demanding and she felt herself go weak in his embrace.

His hands encircled her waist and he pulled her up against him until her toes were barely touching the floor. She wrapped her arms around his neck and surrendered to the sensation of the kiss. Gently he lowered her, her body sliding exquisitely along his until she stood firmly on the floor.

She felt weightless, boneless, as if she had lost all ability to move. Her mind grasped for a coherent thought but was left with bits and pieces of reality—his lips on her neck, the hard ridge of his desire against her stomach, the feel of his breath on her skin.

Suddenly he pulled back and stared into her eyes. When his hands skimmed up her torso until they cupped her face, she waited for another chaste kiss, thinking that he had regained control of his desire. But then he moaned deep in his throat and took her mouth again, as if starved for the taste and feel of her. She felt the last vestige of her reticence melt under the heat of his mouth.

By the time rational thought had again returned to her mind, they were lying on the couch, his body stretched over hers. His palm skimmed along the outside of her thigh, exposed by her twisted skirt. Feelings she had never felt before raced through her body like an explosive chain reaction. His tongue on her lips, his gentle moans, his fingers gripping her knee. She wanted his hands everywhere at once, wanted to lose herself in the pleasure of his exploration. And she desperately wanted to rid herself of her clothes and to tear away his, to feel skin against skin, heat against heat.

As his fingers pulled at her bound hair, she tugged his shirt out of the waistband of his jeans. Suddenly she knew his desperation, his absolute need to touch and feel, for that same drive was now within her. Hesitantly she slid her hands beneath his shirt until her fingertips brushed along his back.

He dragged his mouth from hers and shuddered. "Do you know what your touch does to me?"

He pressed his hips into hers and she could feel his rigid erection through the barrier of their clothes. Her hands moved back to his waist and she urged him on until her skirt was twisted around her waist and he lay cradled between her thighs. His face was buried in the curve of her neck and they rocked gently against each other until he drew a long, shaky breath.

Placing his hands on either side of her head, he pushed up and away from her, just far enough to meet her gaze. "How can I want you so much?" he asked, his brow furrowed in confusion. "What kind of spell have you cast on me? If you tell me it's magic, I'll believe you."

His soft words sank into her hazy mind by degrees and she couldn't deny the dagger of guilt that ripped into her conscience. How could she possibly take pleasure from such a blatant manipulation? It was like stealing from a sleeping man! A torrent of self-recrimination washed over her and for a moment she wanted to drown in it, to put an end to the experiment. She had her answer, she knew how the potion still affected him, so why couldn't she stop? Why did she want more?

"Susannah?"

The sound of her name on his lips startled her out of the depths of her thoughts. She found herself staring at him mutely.

"What's wrong?" he asked.

"I—I can't do this," she said, her voice quivering with emotion. "I'm sorry." With that, she pushed at his chest and scrambled out from under him. She retreated to the fireplace, where she frantically straightened her clothes. He growled in frustration and she turned to find him lying on his back with his arm over his eyes.

"Please, don't be angry," she pleaded.

He pulled his arm away and looked at her. His gaze was clear and lucid. Gone was the passion she had seen there just moments ago.

"I'm not," he replied in a gentle voice. He pushed himself off the couch, then grabbed his jacket from the chair. After he shrugged into it, he stood silently for a long moment, studying her.

Slowly he crossed the room to stand before her. He brought his hand to her cheek. "I can wait, Susannah. I haven't had much experience at it, but I'm willing to give it my best. And when you're ready, I'll be there."

She stood rooted to the spot long after he had promised to call her the next day, long after he had walked out the front door. Branded by the heat from his fingers, she fought the shame that threatened to engulf her. Her mind wandered back to the first time they had met on a snowy street nearly a month ago.

He had asked her that night on the pier about fate and she had told him she didn't believe in fate. Now, she had cause to wonder.

THE RACQUETBALL ricocheted off the right wall and Jay lunged for the shot. He caught it just before it hit the floor and sent it into the corner, where it flew out at a vicious angle. He stepped aside as Mitch tried to make the shot, but his friend was a second too late and a foot too short to salvage a play.

"Game, set and match," Jay said, tossing his racquet up in the air and catching it behind his back.

Mitch rifled the ball at Jay's feet and Jay dodged it. "I'll beat you at least once before you go back to Baltimore," Mitch growled.

"If I had to wait for you to beat me, I'd have to take up permanent residence here," Jay chided.

Mitch shook his head. "I thought you were hell-bent to get out of this provincial town and back to the East Coast. Those were your exact words, weren't they?"

Jay grabbed a towel from outside the door to the racquetball court and wrapped it around his neck. "I am. But it's not so bad here. My stay has become a lot more interesting since I met Susannah Hart."

Jay had to admit he was developing a real fondness for Dr. Hart. She was fun to be with, even though she took herself a bit too seriously. Though her steadfast reserve had become a major frustration for him, her reticence captivated his curiosity and he found himself content to merely chip away at her shell whenever he could. He had been amazed to glimpse an enchanting woman beneath.

Mitch turned to Jay, a worried look creasing his brow. "Susannah? What's going on between you and Susannah?"

Jay wiped his face with the towel. "We had dinner at the Canterbury Inn and lunch a few times at the University Club. And we've seen four movies in as many nights. Last night, we went to see *Casablanca*. She'd never seen that movie before—can you believe it?"

Introducing Susannah to the world outside her laboratory was proving to be more fun than he had imagined. She'd gotten hooked on Bogart classics and had insisted on seeing one film each evening they had spent together. Though her enthusiasm seemed genuine, Jay wondered if Susannah didn't prefer the movies because they were safe. The crowd, the campus location, the quick ride home didn't allow much time for intimacy.

Until last night. When she had invited him in he had been surprised, but pleased. He had welcomed the opening she had offered, but had sensed her apprehension. One kiss was all that it took. They had stepped to the edge, as they had done many times before, but this time, rather than move away, she had pulled him closer. His taste had been whetted for the sensuous woman hidden behind Susannah's proper facade. She hadn't dropped her defenses completely, but he had seen enough. He was willing to wait for that kind of passion.

"Susannah leads a very insulated life," Mitch replied. "Why didn't you tell me about this sooner?"

Jay picked up the racquetball and idly bounced it off the wall as he spoke. "You were preoccupied with Lauren. Besides, there wasn't much to tell. We've seen each other a few times, that's all." Jay smiled. "You know, I really enjoy being with her."

Mitch's expression tensed.

"And I don't mean *being* with her in the biblical sense," Jay added. "We haven't progressed much past kissing, which is a first for me. But it doesn't seem to matter. She's a fascinating woman. And she's sort of shy and nervous around me. I like that. I don't always have to be perfectly charming when I'm around her."

"Sounds like you're hooked," Mitch said.

Jay stopped bouncing the ball and shrugged. "Maybe I am. But I seriously doubt it. I'll be leaving for Baltimore at the end of May and who knows where we'll be by then."

"Well, don't get too hooked," Mitch warned.

Jay turned to face his friend. "What's that supposed to mean?"

Mitch shrugged noncommittally.

"Do you have something to say?" Jay asked. "I know you're not keen on me dating Susannah, but I've been a perfect gentleman. There's nothing for you to worry about."

"I'm not worried about Susannah," Mitch replied. "I'm worried about you."

Jay yanked off his wet T-shirt and dropped it on top of the towel. "Me? Don't be," Jay said. "I'm a big boy and I can take care of myself."

"Maybe so, but there's something you don't know about Susannah. I think it would be best to tell you now, before you get too involved. If you find out later, knowing your temper, it will only be worse for Susannah."

"So spit it out, Mitch," Jay said with a laugh. "What deep, dark secret is Susannah Hart keeping from me?"

"Remember when I thought she was working on research at the faculty reception?"

"Yeah, but you were wrong. She was just out for a night of fun. Looking back on it, I don't think it had anything to do with professional research. And if it did, what harm could a little incognito social observation cause?"

"Well, there's a little more to it than benign observation. She's working on research dealing with pheromones."

"Pheromones? What's that, like hormones?"

"Not exactly. Pheromones are odor lures that attract members of the opposite sex. Susannah and Lauren are working on a formula for a love potion and I'm pretty certain that they're testing their potion on you."

Jay laughed. "Do you have any idea how crazy that sounds? Mitch, if you don't want me to date Susannah, just come right out and say so."

Mitch leaned back against the wall and slowly slid down it until he was sitting on the floor. He rubbed his face with his hands and sighed. "I was over at Lauren's place last night and she had some papers scattered on the floor. I picked them up and read them. I was curious.

They were field reports in Susannah's handwriting on a research subject referred to as 'JB.' The field-test locations match the locations of your dates. They're testing this love potion on you, Beaumont. I'm sure of it."

A stab of anger pierced Jay's chest. What was Mitch saying? That Susannah's interest in him was purely professional? That she was playing him for a fool? He calmed his temper and put on an air of casual indifference. "Did you ask Lauren about what you found? What did she say?"

Mitch shook his head. "I don't think she intended for me to see the papers. She was asleep on the couch when I got to her apartment. I thought I'd do her a favor and clean up, but . . ."

Jay stared at Mitch for a long moment, then shook his head. "I don't believe this! Even if she was working on a love potion, there's no way it would have any effect on me."

"No? You seem to have taken a very strong liking to Susannah without much encouragement. And you have to admit, she's not the type you're usually attracted to."

"Come on! You actually believe she's made a love potion that works?"

"I know Susannah. If anyone can do it, she can. And with the way you're acting, I'd say she's succeeded."

"Yeah, right! I can take her or leave her. I'm not in love with her. Not by any stretch of the imagination."

Mitch crossed his arms over his knees and hung his head. "I wish I could say the same about Lauren. Hell, for all I know, she's using this potion on me!"

"You think what's going on between you and Lauren is part of this experiment, too?"

"I don't think so, but I'm not sure. I care about Lauren, and I'm willing to give her the benefit of the doubt.

She'll tell me about her work sooner or later, and then I'll have to decide whether what we've got is worth anything." He paused. "What are you going to do about Susannah? Are you going to let on that you know?"

Jay shook his head. "No. If she's waiting around for a declaration of love, she'll be waiting a long time. I'm not about to give her the satisfaction. As far as I'm concerned, this experiment is over."

7

SUSANNAH STOOD on the observation deck over the swimming pool and watched the noontime swimmers complete their laps. Lunch hour for the past three days had been spent at the pool, waiting for Jay Beaumont to appear. It had been nearly a week and a half since they had been to the movies together and his parting promise to call her had gone unfulfilled. Susannah was now satisfied that she knew the limits of the potion's residual effect. Without constant use, Jay Beaumont's interest had diminished.

She took a deep breath and gulped back the lump lodged in her throat. The emotional roller coaster she had been riding for the past ten days had hit another valley. A sting of self-reproach shot through her. How much longer was she going to pretend that Jay meant nothing to her? She had ignored her feelings for him too long and now they threatened to erupt in a maelstrom of recriminations and regrets.

The past week had been torture, waiting for him to call, hoping to bump into him on campus. He intruded on her thoughts at every turn, until she was certain she was going mad. His touch, his scent, the rich sound of his voice, every memory they shared was replayed again and again, until she finally was forced to admit the truth.

She was thoroughly infatuated with Jay Beaumont.

How it had happened, she wasn't sure. All she knew was that her personal feelings and her professional goals had somehow tangled, until it was impossible to distinguish one from the other. She wanted Jay Beaumont. But why?

Was it simply a response to *his* response? The potion had transformed him into an attentive suitor. But whether the pheromone was worn by Susannah Hart or someone equally unsuitable, Jay's reactions would have been the same. His feelings for her were a result of scientific manipulation. Once the catalyst was gone, those feelings would evaporate. So wouldn't logic dictate that what she was feeling was not real, either?

Susannah bit back a curse. Logic. She had always been able to reason her way through any situation with the help of simple logic. But lately, when it came to her cognitive skills, they seemed to take a sudden sabbatical whenever Jay Beaumont stepped into the room.

She glanced back down at the pool and her eyes were drawn to a figure at the far end. In one sharp movement, Jay dived into the pool, his finely muscled body splitting the water like a knife. He came up for air somewhere near the middle, then began a strong crawl to the edge. She watched him swim several more lengths as she gathered her courage. Then she pulled the vial of potion from her pocket and applied it liberally on her neck and wrists. Drawing a deep breath, she started for the stairs that led to the pool level. After a ten-day delay, it was time for the field test to resume.

Her footsteps echoed in the huge cavernous room that housed the pool. The smell of chlorine tickled her nose and the splashing sounds from the swimmers set her nerves on edge. She slowly made her way to the end of the pool and waited for Jay to complete another lap. As he swam nearer, her heart began to pound wildly, but then he completed a perfect flip turn at her feet and began his trip to the other end. Susannah stifled a moan. There was no way he'd be able to detect the potion with his nose underwater.

She hurried along the edge of the pool and made it to the opposite end with two strokes to spare, but again he executed a quick turn and began to swim away from her. Susannah's confusion rose. She knew he'd seen her! Twice, he looked right into her face as he came up for air, but he gave no sign of recognition. He was deliberately ignoring her. But why? She stalked to the opposite end of the pool. If he didn't acknowledge her this time, she would make him.

Susannah stepped up to the edge, bent down and waited for his approach, prepared to tap him on the shoulder. His pace had slowed considerably, until he seemed to be treading water in the middle of the pool. She tapped her foot impatiently and waited for Jay to complete his lap. When he reached the edge of the pool she was ready.

Gingerly she reached out to touch him, determined to put this ridiculous game to an end, but he slipped away. She made a frantic grab for his ankle, but Jay was a much stronger swimmer than she had anticipated. As he pushed off the wall, she felt her balance pulled from beneath her. Arms flailing, she tried to regain her footing, but it was no use.

With a monumental splash, she hit the surface of the water and promptly sank to the bottom, her clothes weighing her down like an anchor. She had nearly resigned herself to drowning, when strong hands circled her waist and lifted her. In the next instant she was sitting on the edge of the pool, sputtering for breath, her hair plastered in front of her eyes and water puddling around her.

He stood before her in waist-deep water, his brow raised questioningly. "Dr. Hart. We meet again. This time it *must* be fate." His voice was dry and his smile cynical.

As oxygen slowly filled her lungs, mortification seeped into her thoughts. She was tempted to jump back into the pool and wait out the embarrassment on the bottom of the deep end. She tried to speak, but then stopped herself, at a complete loss for an excuse. How could she hope to restart the field test now? After her quick dip, the potion was completely washed away. There had to at least be a way to salvage her dignity and her research. But with a half-naked Jay Beaumont standing in front of her, she found it impossible to think clearly.

Her mind whirled with uncontrolled impulses. She found herself fascinated by the beads of water that glistened on his chest, by the sheen of his wet skin and the curl of his damp hair against his neck. How long she stared at him she wasn't sure, but when she finally regained control of herself, she realized it had been far too long.

She brushed her stringy hair out of her eyes, then picked up a corner of her gray poplin trench coat and wrung it out. The raincoat was waterproof, but it had done nothing to protect her during her deep-water disaster.

"I'm sorry to disturb your swim, Professor Beaumont," she said as nonchalantly as possible, "but I was wondering if you'd care to have lunch with me today."

He braced his arms on the pool deck and pulled himself out of the water to sit beside her. "A phone call would have been simpler," he replied. "And drier."

She nodded mutely as she let her eyes wander down his chest until they reached his narrow waist. There

wasn't much standing between Jay Beaumont and na-
kedness, and her imagination was quickly doing away
with the small scrap of fabric that was. Her gaze jumped
back to his face, where she found a smug smile curling
his lips. "I—I didn't plan to fall in," she replied defen-
sively.

"I'm sure you didn't." He slicked his hair back with his
fingers, then leaned back and stared across the pool. "Is
that really why you're here? To invite me to lunch?"

"I was just passing by on my way to...to the other side
of campus and when I saw you, I ... well, you know the
rest."

"Yes. Well, I'm afraid I don't have time for lunch today," he replied.

She sensed an undercurrent of tension in his voice.

"Oh ... that's too bad," Susannah said, gazing down
at her feet. She noticed that she had lost a shoe and upon
further searching spotted it on the bottom of the pool. "I
just thought that maybe ..."

They sat in silence for a long time and suddenly the
absurdity of the situation began to sink in. Susannah
Hart, soaked to the skin and completely out of her element, was asking—no begging—Jay Beaumont to have
lunch with her. What was she doing here? Without the
potion, he was showing absolutely no interest in her.
Who would? She probably looked worse than a drowned
rodent. Biting back a moan of frustration, she straightened her coat and struggled to her feet.

Susannah noticed that a smile twitched at the corners
of Jay's mouth as he followed her movements. He was
actually enjoying this! Glancing around, she found most
of the swimmers gathered at the edge of the pool sharing
in Jay's amusement. She'd been humiliated enough and
now it was time to make a graceful exit.

"You probably want to finish your swim." She paused and sniffed. "And now that I've seen for myself that you're in good health, there's no reason to stay."

He stood up beside her. "Good health?"

Regretting the impulse to speak her mind, she trained her voice to indifference. "When you didn't call, I just assumed that you had been hit by a bus or contracted malaria or that some other terrible situation had befallen you. What other reason would there be to break a promise?" She pushed a strand of hair out of her eyes, then tugged on the belt of her coat. "Now, I really must be going." She turned away, but he grabbed her by the elbow.

"Wait a minute. When did I make any promises?"

She turned back to him and raised her chin defiantly. "I must have misunderstood. When you said you'd call me tomorrow, I just assumed that you meant the day after today, when today was a week ago last Friday. Unless, of course, you literally meant tomorrow, which raises the philosophical question of whether tomorrow ever really comes and whether you intended to call me at all." Susannah stopped suddenly, realizing by his widening grin that he still wasn't taking her seriously. It was no wonder. In addition to looking like an idiot and acting like an idiot, she was now beginning to sound like one.

"What do you want me to say?" he asked.

"Nothing," she shot back.

He rubbed his hands along her upper arms and smiled. An uncontrolled shiver raced through her and her teeth began to chatter. "Are you sure you wouldn't rather get out of those wet clothes and into something dry?"

She pulled out of his grasp. "I'm fine."

Taking her hand, he led her over to a bench against the wall. She limped along with one shoe, wondering if she should just kick the other off or pretend nothing was amiss. She decided to pretend.

He pushed her down onto the bench, then walked over and grabbed a couple of towels from a cart and, to her relief, wrapped one around his waist. Now maybe she'd be able to think! He handed her the second, then sat down beside her on the bench.

There was a long silence before he drew a deep breath and began to speak. "Susannah, you're a wonderful woman and any man would be lucky to have you in his life, but . . ."

She could sense what was coming. He'd obviously had plenty of practice with this particular speech. His execution was flawless, just the proper dose of self-reproach and regret in his voice. Her heart twisted at his words and she tried not to let her disappointment show. This was all to be expected, she rationalized.

After a period of intense infatuation, the brain often develops an immunity to the lust-inducing chemicals, Dr. Gruber had written. *Some may even develop an addiction to the lust rush, seeking out new targets and more intense chemical reactions as old relationships falter and fade.*

Could Jay be one of Dr. Gruber's lust junkies? From all she'd heard of his past, he certainly fit the profile. And if he was, there was little chance of maintaining his interest without ever-increasing applications of the potion. Susannah felt her dreams slipping through her fingers. There had to be a way to put this field test back on track! She was so close.

Attainment of the human male's conquest severely reduces the intensity of infatuation. By maintaining an in-

different attitude during the chase, the female can extend the initial period of infatuation. She did have one advantage. This game he was playing was well documented in research and she knew exactly how to counteract it.

"I just think things were moving a little too fast for us," he concluded. "Too fast for me. I'm just not ready to make a commitment to one woman."

"I see," she murmured.

"So, I think it would be best if we didn't see each other for a while. I'll be going back East in another month or two and you have your work."

Susannah calmly folded her hands in her lap and smiled brightly. "You're right. I couldn't agree more," she replied. "There is no reason for us to continue seeing each other."

"What?" Jay seemed genuinely taken aback.

She obviously wasn't responding the way he had hoped. Yet *his* response was as predictable as the sunrise in the morning. Susannah sent a silent prayer of gratitude to Dr. Gruber and her insightful research, then turned and patted Jay's hand sympathetically. "But of course we can still be friends," she said.

He frowned, clearly baffled at her easy comeback. She had taken the words right out of his mouth and the wind right out of his sails. "Well . . . sure," he agreed. "It's just that we *were* moving toward something more serious."

"We were?" She gave him an innocent look. "Hmm. I must have missed that."

Jay regarded her suspiciously. "Are you saying what happened between us meant nothing to you?"

"What *did* happen between us? We had dinner and lunch a few times. We went to the movies. You kissed me,

what, three times? I don't see how that constitutes anything more than a friendship."

"A friendship? Come on. There was more to us than
friendship. Or do all your male friends enjoy the same
passion?"

"Passion? There was passion? My, how could I have
missed *that?*"

Jay shot up out of his spot and paced back and forth
before her. "So what went on between us meant nothing
to you?" he demanded.

"Was it supposed to mean something?"

She watched him, catching an intriguing glimpse of a
well-muscled thigh beneath the towel as he walked. For
an impetuous moment, she felt an urge to reach out and
snatch the towel away, then chastised herself for her un-
curbed fantasizing. Good Lord, what *was* this fascination she had with his body? He had the same anatomical
features as every other male on the planet, but they were
assembled in such a way as to drive even the most de-
mure female to blatant ogling.

"Yes!" He paused, then frowned. "I mean, no."

She sighed, then stood up, certain that she had won the
game, if not the match. It would be wise to quit while she
was ahead, before her disobedient hormones decided to
even the odds a bit. "I'm afraid you've read much more
into this friendship than is truly there, Professor Beaumont. You're right. It would be best if we didn't see each
other again." She held out her hand and he took it. When
she shook it firmly, his eyes reflected his shock. "Good
luck with your book." Then she tipped her chin up
proudly and began to walk away, trying hard to maintain a regal bearing with only one shoe.

"Wait a minute," he called.

She turned back to him with a questioning look.

He opened his mouth to speak, then snapped it shut. A second later he opened it again, then sighed and shook his head. She thought she heard him utter Mitch's name amid a string of softly muttered curses. "What about lunch tomorrow?" he finally asked.

She felt a glow of supreme satisfaction. "Would that be the real tomorrow or the philosophical tomorrow?"

"Do you want to have lunch with me or not?" he growled.

Susannah gave him sweet smile. "I'm afraid I don't have time for lunch tomorrow. Why don't you call me and we'll find another time?"

With that she turned on her one remaining heel and limped toward the women's locker room. First she would get out of these wet clothes. And then she would call Lauren at the lab and have her bring her some dry clothes. And after that, she would revel in the fact that for the first time since her field test had begun, she had managed to maintain perfect control over herself—and her subject.

"LUNCH TODAY would be fine," Susannah replied, her fingers gripping her office phone. She glanced up and caught Lauren's grin and gave her a thumbs-up sign. "Yes, a half hour would be fine. I'll see you then." She carefully put the receiver in the cradle.

"Professor Beaumont?" Lauren asked.

"Who else?" Susannah said. "It seems he's had cause to reconsider his original plan to dump me. After a brief lapse in the field test, we are back on track. Thank goodness for the residual qualities of the potion and for Dr. Gruber's insight into the male mind."

Lauren nodded distractedly. "Susannah, don't you find it odd that we didn't see any residual effect from the potion during our research with Max and Minnie?"

"Odd?" Susannah considered the question, then shrugged. "Not really. We weren't expecting any so we didn't look for any. Some of the greatest scientific discoveries have been made by mistake." But Lauren's observation did warrant further thought. And further documentation.

"It think it might be a good idea if I did some backup research in that area," Lauren said. "I've got a discussion group to cover for Derwin next hour. Dr. Curtis sent the little worm off to Washington, D.C., on some academic adventure. I'll get started later this afternoon."

Susannah glanced up. "What? Oh, yes. I do think it would be a good idea to do some additional research. I'll see if I can borrow Max and Minnie for a few weeks."

Lauren stood and grabbed her jacket from the back of her chair. "Good. I'll see you after your lunch with the bachelor professor." She placed her palms on Susannah's desk and smiled teasingly. "Be careful out there. There are wolves lurking in the woods and I wouldn't want a big bad one named Jay to gobble you up for lunch."

Susannah forced a laugh. "Never!" she cried. "I have complete control over this experiment. If anyone should be careful it's Professor Beaumont. You see, I've developed a foolproof trap for wolves and I'm determined to catch this one."

"You may catch him, Susannah," Lauren countered, "but will you be able to let him go afterward?"

She stared at her lab assistant for a long moment, unable to come up with a flippant response. Why did the prospect of losing Jay cause such a gnawing ache so deep inside her? Wasn't it only a few days ago that he had tried to put an end to their relationship? He had no feelings for her beyond those that the potion brought forth and it was about time she came to grips with that simple fact. No matter how much she wanted to believe differently, Jay Beaumont could never love her. She was wasting her time mooning over a man she could never have.

"Susannah, what's wrong?"

Lauren's words interrupted her thoughts and she snapped to attention. "Nothing," she replied. "I—I was just thinking about my lecture notes for class tomorrow morning, that's all."

"Are you sure you're all right?" Lauren asked.

"Of course, why wouldn't I be?" Susannah swallowed hard. "You'd better get going or you'll be late for class. And I've got to get ready for my lunch date with Professor Beaumont."

"All right. I'll see you later," Lauren said, a frown creasing her brow. She walked to the door and gave Susannah one more backward glance before she left the office.

At the sound of the door closing, Susannah breathed a sigh of relief, then stood and walked to the window. Outside, the trees were beginning to bud and the wind blew soft and warm. All over campus, students were restless, feeling the stirrings that spring brought. Like so many before them, beyond recorded history, they would search out a partner and play out the rites of spring. Again and again the cycle would be repeated, and from it would come the next generation and the next, on and on. For the first time in her life, she understood the undeniable urge to seek out a mate, to pay heed to the imprint left in her genes by her cavewoman ancestors.

With a softly spoken admonishment, she spun away from the window. If she wasn't careful, she'd start believing in all the romantic silliness that people insisted on attaching to spring! What could anyone possibly find romantic in a basic chemical reaction that took place after the vernal equinox?

She yanked open her desk drawer and removed a vial of the potion. "Love in a bottle," she murmured to herself as she applied a dose. "Just a little dab here and a little dab there and a woman can have any man she wants."

A sharp knock sounded at the door and Susannah jumped. A quick glance at her watch proved that Jay was ten minutes early. She placed the vial back in her desk drawer, then smoothed her skirt before calmly walking to the door. But it wasn't Jay Beaumont who waited on the other side. Derwin Erwin stood in the doorway, a rapturous grin on his face.

"I'm back!" he said triumphantly, his voice cracking on the last word. "Aren't you happy to see me?"

His words took a moment to register and then Susannah realized that she hadn't seen Derwin in more than two weeks. Not since their bizarre encounter at the Canterbury Inn. She faintly recalled Lauren's comment about his absence, but couldn't remember the details. She had just assumed he had finally resolved whatever psychological problems had been provoking him and had been deliberately avoiding her out of embarrassment. He didn't seem the least bit embarrassed now.

"You're back? I didn't realize you were gone," she replied warily.

"Dr. Curtis sent me to a symposium at Georgetown University. I didn't think it would ever end, but here I am."

"Yes, I see that. I appreciate your informing me of your return, Mr. Erwin. Now, if you'll excuse me, I have—"

Derwin pushed his way past her into her office, then turned to her. "I've missed you, Susannah. You're all I've thought about these past few weeks. You and the perilous plight of the South American tree slug." He gazed into her eyes, then frowned. "I thought about *you* more, though," he added.

Susannah closed the door partway, unwilling to shut off her only means of escape but determined to keep their conversation from curious ears. Slowly she approached Derwin. His eyes were glazed and his enraptured expression was reminiscent of a love-struck moose. She studied his face, listened to his rapid respiration and watched as he grew uncomfortable under her stare. "Derwin," she quietly began. "Have you been using too much of that nasal inhalant again?"

He answered her question with a perplexed expression.

"Why are you here?" she asked.

He withdrew a handkerchief from his pocket and wiped his nose nervously. "Susannah, I . . . Susannah, we . . ."

"Just tell me what's on your mind."

Suddenly, without the slightest warning, he wrapped his arms around her, pinning her arms to her sides in an excruciating hug and lifting her from the floor. "Susannah, I can't fight this any longer. I know you want me. Don't deny it. We belong together."

She tried to squirm out of his grasp, but it was no use. Derwin Erwin was a man driven by pure lust, endowing him with a superhuman strength. She kicked at his shins, but he seemed unaware of any pain. "Derwin, put me down!" she demanded. He only hugged her more tightly.

"I know what you're thinking," he said. "I'm too young for you. And I'm smarter than you are. But we can't let IQ get in the way of true love." He returned her to the floor and she drew a badly needed breath. "Marry me, Susannah, and have my children."

A wave of revulsion ran through her at the thought of procreating with Derwin Erwin. "Don't say that," she said. "Don't even think it! I have no intention of letting this—this infatuation continue, Mr. Erwin."

Infatuation? The word echoed in her mind. No, it couldn't be! Or could it? Could Derwin really be infatuated with her? All the signs had been there from the beginning, but she had just been too wrapped up with Jay to see them. What did this mean?

He held fast to her as she backed toward her desk. All she could think of was getting to the phone and dialing the campus police. Before she could examine this strange twist in her research, someone had to save her from this lust-crazed lunatic!

"Don't fight it, Susannah. I can see it in your eyes." She felt the edge of her desk against her backside and reached behind her to find the phone. "You want me and I want you." He was leaning closer and she turned away until she was half lying across her desk. She had the phone in her hand and was about to reach for the dial, when suddenly she was free of his bone-crushing embrace.

She rolled off the desk and back onto her feet to find Jay standing in the middle of her office. He had Derwin trapped in the crook of his arm in a rather effective headlock.

"What do you think you're doing?" Derwin shouted. "Let me go, you Neanderthal."

"Would you care to explain this, Susannah?"

Jay's voice was smooth and oh-so condescending, and she felt anger burn a path through her body. Explanations? Who was he to be demanding explanations? Derwin was right. He was acting like an overbearing caveman. "I don't owe you, or anyone for that matter, an explanation," she replied calmly.

"That's the way to tell him, darling," Derwin called from under Jay's arm.

"Shut up, Erwin!" they said simultaneously.

"I will not—"

Derwin finished his sentence with a yelp as Jay tightened his hold.

"Let him go, Jay."

He watched her through narrowed eyes, his jaw tense, his expression hard. Then, with a harsh laugh, he released Derwin and the skinny graduate student fell to the floor. In a flash Derwin scrambled to her side and placed his arm around her shoulder. She slapped at his hand and stepped out of his grasp.

"So this is the guy," Jay said scornfully.

"The guy?" Susannah asked. "What guy?"

"The guy you dumped me for," Jay said. "Jeez, Susannah, look at him. Do you really want him more than me?"

A hysterical laugh escaped her throat at Jay's ridiculous take on the situation, a laugh that she couldn't seem to stop. She tried to bring herself under control, but for the first time in her life, her emotions got the best of her. Before long, tears rolled down her cheeks and she held her aching sides, trying to regain her composure. Jay and Derwin gaped at her, both of them struck dumb by her behavior.

Something had gone dreadfully wrong with her research. Somehow she had managed to attract both Jay and Derwin! Imagine, plain old Susannah Hart, caught in a romantic tug-of-war between two egotistical, overbearing males. Though they had very little in common, both Jay and Derwin seemed to share the driving need to possess her. The thought caused another round of laughter. Her potion worked! It really worked! It just worked a little too well.

"Go ahead, Susannah," Derwin urged. "Tell this barbarian how you feel. Tell him you're in love with me."

"In your dreams, you pencil-necked dweeb," Jay shot back.

"Sticks and stones can—"

"Stop it!" Susannah shouted between gasps for breath. "Derwin, I want you to leave. We'll discuss this later."

"But, darling—"

"Now, Mr. Erwin," Susannah warned. "And please, don't call me 'darling'!"

"Yes, dear," Derwin murmured as Susannah shut the office door behind him.

She turned around to face Jay, taking in his angry scowl. This field test had become a regular soap opera, complete with a melodramatic love triangle. But this bizarre turn of events was significant. She'd already received a profession of love from her unintentional research subject, Derwin. All she needed now was the same from Jay Beaumont and the field test could be deemed an unqualified success.

"I think it's time we had a little talk, Professor Beaumont. And maybe we should start by discussing your behavior."

"*My* behavior?" Jay asked. "I wasn't the one doing the horizontal mambo with Derwin Erwin! I thought we had a lunch date and I show up to find you in the arms of a geeky kid. You're the one who owes me an explanation, Susannah."

Susannah slowly walked to her desk and sat down in her chair. This was all quite interesting. Jay Beaumont was showing very distinct symptoms of jealousy—a state of high emotion that often led to a realization of love. She was so close to the culmination of all her work. But beneath her calm facade, her excitement was tempered with fear as Lauren's words came back to her. Would she be able to walk away from Jay Beaumont with no regrets? Would she be able to put an end to her field test and then go on with her life as if Jay had never entered it?

"After our conversation at the pool, I thought you had decided to put an end to any romantic future for us," she said softly. "Correct me if I'm wrong, but your behavior seems to be bordering on . . . jealousy? Not a normal reaction for a mere friend."

"What? Me?" he gasped. "Jealous of Derwin Erwin?"

Susannah nodded, watching the play of emotions cross his handsome features.

"No way, sweetheart," he muttered.

"Hmm. I see. Then maybe you could offer an explanation of your own for your intense reaction."

Jay clenched his jaw and glared at her distrustfully. "What do you want me to say, Susannah?"

"What do *you* want to say, Professor Beaumont?"

With an angry shout of frustration, Jay slammed his palms down on her desk. "Why do you always answer a question with another question? Sometimes you sound more like a shrink than the woman I—"

Susannah's heart jumped nervously. So close, so very close. *Say it, Jay,* her mind begged. *Say it, so I can put you out of my life.* "The woman you what?"

Jay stared at her for a long time, then shook his head and smiled sardonically. "I have to go." He pushed himself away from her desk and walked toward the door. He paused for a moment, then turned back to her, grasping the edge of the door with a white-knuckled hand. "I'll call you," he said in a deceptively even voice.

"I won't count on it," she replied against a rising flood of frustration.

"Then that would be your second mistake, Dr. Hart." With that, he turned and walked out the door, leaving her to wonder just what her first mistake had been.

DAMN! What the hell was she doing to him?

Jay shoved his shoulder against the front door of Science Hall and stepped outside. As he walked toward his office, he yanked his tie loose and unbuttoned the top two buttons of his shirt. Suddenly he felt the need to get away, to leave the campus and Susannah Hart as far behind as possible. Or at least far enough away to think rationally. The woman had an uncanny ability to tie him into knots even a seasoned sailor couldn't untangle.

Fifteen minutes later he was on his way out of town, his suit jacket tossed in the back seat of the Jag, his tie hooked around the rearview mirror and his sleeves rolled to his elbows. The wind whipped through the open car windows as he sped along the highway to the far side of the lake. He drew a deep breath, determined to drive the image of Susannah Hart right from his mind.

Jealous? Jay Beaumont? Cynthia had taken every jealous bone in his body, along with half their worldly possessions, in the divorce settlement, leaving him immune to any emotions tinged with green. Jealousy was only a cruel reminder of his stupidity, and an emotion that required a level of commitment that he was unprepared to offer. But if he wasn't jealous, why was he so angry?

He was nearly certain that Susannah wasn't attracted to Derwin Erwin, though Derwin's motives were more than clear. A nooner in Susannah's office was obviously top on his agenda. A fierce rush of rage pulsed through him at the thought of Erwin's hands on Susannah, so overwhelming that he pulled the car over to the side of the road and skidded to a stop.

What the hell was wrong with him? His hands gripped the steering wheel until his fingers went numb. Then, with a resigned sigh, he leaned back into the soft leather seat and raked his fingers through his hair.

Give it up, Beaumont. Though he had tried to deny her hold on him, he somehow knew that facing the truth was inevitable. The ice that had encased his heart had begun to thaw the night he'd found her beneath a halo of light in the library basement. It hadn't taken long to realize what other men had overlooked. Susannah was an extraordinary woman, a woman of contrasts, skittish and shy, yet filled with a steely inner strength and determination that rivaled his own.

For years he had unconsciously gathered the specifications for his ideal woman. And every time a female had come close to meeting them, he would add another requirement, convincing himself that perfection was simply unattainable. Now he could see his ploy for what it truly was. A clever excuse to avoid commitment. And a convoluted plan to bypass the pain that commitment eventually brought. But Susannah was different. When he looked into her eyes, he saw not simply another incarnation of his ex-wife, but a woman worth . . . Jay exhaled slowly. Worth what?

He squeezed his eyes shut and and tried to focus on the faint message drifting in and out of his consciousness. *Worth loving,* his mind softly stated. *Worth risking his heart for, worth giving his life to.*

Jay's eyes snapped open and he stared out the windshield at a passing car. But what about her research, her manipulation? Susannah Hart was no different from Cynthia, using him as a means to an end. How could he possibly love her after learning of her true motives?

Jay guided the Jag back onto the road and deftly worked through the gears until the car was cruising again. He tried to clear his head by concentrating on the sounds of the engine and the feel of the road beneath him. But try as he might, her image kept intruding on his thoughts. By the time he'd turned off the main road and onto the narrow drive that led to his property, he had decided not to fight the anger anymore. He would have to deal with Susannah Hart and her conniving, one way or another.

He parked the car in front of the boat shed and waited patiently for the anger to return. But when it didn't, he wasn't surprised. After all, the idea of a love potion was about as believable as the legend of a fountain of youth. And the notion that he might fall under the effects of this potion was just as outlandish.

He had managed quite nicely to fall in love with Susannah Hart all on his own, despite his very best efforts to the contrary. Her silly experiment meant nothing to him, beyond the fact that it had brought them together. That was all that mattered now. But if he wasn't careful, it could tear them apart.

All the qualities he had come to admire in her were the same qualities that were sure to work against him—her single-minded purpose, her dedication to her work and her stubborn refusal to admit failure. Susannah Hart believed that love could only be found in the bottom of a test tube. Jay knew she was wrong. And standing between them were reams of research reports and years of hard work.

Jay stepped out of the car and walked to the shed. He opened the lock and pulled the doors open, then walked into the dim interior. The tarp-covered boat was illuminated by streams of sunlight that filtered through the gaps in the weathered wood siding. Slowly he walked the length of the hull, running his hand along the smooth surface.

He had just one hope, one chance to make this work, and that was to force Susannah to realize the flaws in her theory. Admitting that he loved her would get him nothing but a brief footnote in her final published research paper and a quick farewell. But if he could get Susannah to admit that she loved him, then they might have a chance. She would have no choice but to admit that her theories were wrong.

He had discovered a woman beneath the serious scientific veneer of Susannah Hart. But transforming scientist into seductress might be more than even he could handle.

8

"DERWIN ATTACKED you?" Lauren's exclamation rattled
the glass-doored lab cabinets.

"Maybe 'attack' is too strong a word," Susannah replied calmly. "I was never really concerned for my safety.
Derwin just got overly amorous. Either way, I'm positive that the potion is having some effect on him as well
as Jay."

The color drained from Lauren's face and she slowly
lowered herself onto a lab stool. "Wh-why would you say
that?"

Susannah noticed her lab assistant's distraught expression and reached over to give her hand an encour-
aging squeeze. "Derwin admitted that he was in love with
me. In fact, he thinks we ought to get married and have
a bunch of little Erwins." Susannah made a silly face, but
Lauren didn't respond to her good humor. "This is nothing to be upset about. A minor glitch, that's all. We've
shown highly positive results from both Jay and Derwin. We just need to work out a few of the kinks."

"Susannah, I think I should tell you th—"

"Don't worry. Whatever caused this deviation couldn't
be predicted. We'll just have to deal with it."

"But I—"

"We'll need to take more time to study these aspects of
the potion, of course, before we can ever hope to market
the formulation. But I don't think this should have any
effect on our plans to present our research. Jay is close to

succumbing to the potion and I'll have a definitive result from him after our next meeting."

"How can you be so sure?" Lauren asked.

"I've doubled the potion's strength," Susannah replied.

"You what?"

"I took a small amount of the potion and distilled it. If things go as I predict, the double-strength potion will put Jay over the edge. He'll admit he loves me and our field test will be complete. We can send him back East in a few weeks none the wiser." Susannah tried to inject a note of detachment into her voice, but the thought of Jay leaving Riversbend caused a lump of emotion to choke her voice. She turned away from Lauren and busied herself by arranging clean test tubes in a rack.

"Susannah, is there something you'd like to talk about?"

She shook her head. She'd like nothing better than to tell Lauren everything, to have someone there to understand her dilemma, to help her survive losing Jay. But she was ashamed of her behavior and her inability to maintain a safe scientific distance. And she was reluctant to admit her failure, even to Lauren.

"Are you in love with Jay?"

She spun around to face Lauren, shocked by her assistant's intuitiveness. "No!"

"Are you sure?"

"Yes," Susannah replied emphatically. She gulped down the lump in her throat, but it returned almost instantly. "No," she amended. Her eyes began to water and she forced a tight smile to her lips. "I—I don't know. Oh, Lauren, everything's so confused right now, I'm not sure how I feel. I just want this whole thing to be over with so my life can get back to normal."

162

Love Potion #9Love Potion #9

A tear sprang from the corner of her eye and she angrily brushed it away. "I know there can be no future for us. The only reason he's showing me any attention at all is because of the potion. I just got a little too wrapped up in my research, that's all. I was even starting to believe in all the hearts and flowers and sappy sentiments. Once he's gone, everything will be fine." Though she desperately wanted to believe her own words, Susannah knew it would be a long time before she'd forget Jay.

"You should tell him how you feel."

"Why? It won't make any difference. Without the potion, we could never have any kind of lasting relationship."

"Is that what you want with Jay?"

Susannah bit her lip and nodded. "I think so. But all this time we've spent together has clouded my judgment. Maybe I am in love with him. Or I might just be caught up in an intense infatuation. I guess I won't know for sure until after he's gone. And by then it will be too late to change anything."

"Maybe he'll decide to stay," Lauren said hopefully.

"There's about as much chance of that as there is of Einstein failing an IQ test," she replied. "I'll just need to concentrate on our work and complete the field research as we'd planned."

Lauren drew a deep breath and shifted uncomfortably on the stool. "While you're doing that, I'd like to do some further work on the potion. There's something we've missed and I'd like to find out what it is. Do you have any left in the vial you've been using?"

"Sure," Susannah replied. "I only distilled half of what I had left." She retrieved the vial from a rack on the counter and handed it to Lauren. "You can use this. But what are you looking for?"

Lauren held the test tube up to the light and for a long time stared at the liquid that swirled within it. "I'm not sure yet. But when I find it, I'll let you know." She looked over at Susannah. "I'd better get to work."

"And I've got a final exam to put together," Susannah said, "so I'll leave you to it. I'll be in my office if you need me."

Lauren nodded, already distracted with arranging her lab equipment on the counter. Susannah walked out of the lab and closed the door quietly behind her, then instinctively searched the hallway for any sign of Derwin as she raced toward her office. She was safely locked inside before she noticed the overwhelming scent of flowers.

Turning from the door, Susannah gasped in surprise at the sight that greeted her. Her desk, her cabinets, her bookshelves, every surface was hidden by huge bouquets of flowers. An awestruck sigh escaped her lips as she stepped to the middle of the room. Slowly she turned around, taking in the sights and smells of roses, lilies, daffodils and daisies. They had to be from Jay, she thought as she searched each bouquet for a card. Derwin was too obtuse to think of such a romantic gesture. She found nothing to indicate the sender, until she spied a bottle of champagne hidden behind a large arrangement of irises on her desk. A card dangled from the neck of the bottle: "You were right. Meet me on the dock at the Canterbury at two on Saturday afternoon and I'll make it up to you. Love, J. P.S. Bring the champagne."

Love. Susannah stared long and hard at the word. She was tempted to take the scribbled endearment at face value. Jay had admitted his feelings for her. There was no need to go on with the field test. But a carelessly written sentiment would not do. She needed to hear the words, just once, before she could put an end to this difficult time in her career. Once was all she would have, though she knew she would spend the rest of her life listening to the echo of those three words.

She had three days to prepare for their final meeting and the culmination of the field test. Three days spent imagining the circumstances that would lead to his confession of love. Would she be wrapped in his arms in some four-poster at the Canterbury, numb from his kisses, when he finally said them? Or would they be walking hand in hand along the dock, watching the twinkling lights across a moonlit lake? Or would they be lying on a blanket in some sun-kissed meadow filled with wildflowers?

She could picture it all quite vividly. The warmth of his skin under her palms, the gentle ebb and flow of his breathing against her cheek, the silkiness of his hair between her fingers. His strong hands on her body, his hard mouth against hers. She could imagine him beside her, on top of her, then inside her, and with that image came an overwhelming desire to make the fantasy real.

She shook herself from her dreams and bit back a delicate curse. Yes, she could imagine the incredible passion. The only thing she couldn't imagine was walking away when it was over.

SATURDAY DAWNED clear and warm, a perfect day in early May. Jay stood on the dock at the marina as the sun rose over the eastern shore of the lake and watched as a stationary crane slowly lowered *Osprey* into the water. The sleek twenty-five-foot sloop gleamed in the soft rays of the morning sun, her deck freshly varnished and her fittings highly polished. Jay felt a swell of pride at the results of his careful work. She was a classic beauty brought back to life by gentle, patient hands.

Jay glanced at his watch. He had plenty of time to step the mast, rig the sails and run the lines before he was due on the other side of the lake to meet Susannah. If the brisk breeze from the east held, the sail would take no time. There, beside the dock at the Canterbury Inn, they would christen the boat and take her out for her maiden sail. He couldn't think of anyone else he'd rather share this moment with than Susannah.

In fact, over the past three days he'd found himself wanting to share every detail of his life with her—and wanting to know every detail of hers. Somehow he knew that they were destined to be together. Cynthia had been a minor detour on the road to finding Susannah. Looking back on his marriage, he realized that he had never loved his wife the way he loved Susannah—sometimes with an almost overwhelming intensity like a storm at sea, and at other times with a crystalline awareness as calm as a windless day on the water.

He still found it amazing that he had fallen in love with Susannah the old-fashioned way, without pretense and artifice, without seduction and sex. With Susannah he could be himself, the man he was brought up to be, honest and honorable. It was as if he had come full circle and along the way had indulged in every pleasure known to a dedicated bachelor. But he didn't want that solitary life anymore.

His circle had closed and Susannah was in the middle. Susannah with her dark liquid eyes and her unruly hair, her angelic profile and her perfect body. Susannah with her virginal responses and her sensual undercurrents. He closed his eyes and inhaled the damp morning air, his fingers clenching with the need to touch her.

"She's beautiful."

Jay exhaled slowly. "Yes, she is," he replied, recognizing Mitch's voice. He opened his eyes and turned to his friend.

"I meant the boat," Mitch said.

"And I didn't," Jay said with a smile. He raised his arms over his head, then clasped his hands and stretched sinuously. As he lowered his arms, he fixed his gaze on the far side of the lake.

"Susannah?" Mitch asked.

"Yeah. Susannah."

"How bad?"

He turned to Mitch. "Real bad. I'm in love with her."

Mitch laughed sharply. "Welcome to the club. All we need now is one more stooge and we can replace Larry, Curly and Moe."

"You still think Susannah's potion is at the bottom of this, don't you?"

"Don't you?"

Jay bent to pick up a pebble from the dock. "*If*—and this is just pure speculation now—Susannah *has* developed a love potion, and *if* this potion works, then I guess it might change a few things. But it's going to take a lot more than scientific mumbo jumbo to convince me that my nose is what made me fall in love with Susannah." He drew his arm back and whipped the pebble out across the glittering surface of the lake.

"So you're not angry about this?"

He shrugged. "I was at first, but then I realized just what this whole silly experiment brought me." Jay laughed. "As far as I'm concerned, Susannah can use me for any kind of sexual research she wants, as long as I get a lifetime contract as her number one lab rat."

"So what's the plan? Are you going to marry her?"

Jay frowned. "I've considered asking, but I think any proposal now might scare Susannah away. For all I know, she hasn't realized her feelings for me yet. I'm pretty sure they're there, but I think she's trying like hell to ignore them. The first thing I need to do is get Susannah to give in to her desires. Completely. Then we'll be on even ground and we can decide what to do from there."

"You're going to seduce Susannah?"

"I've faced up to my feelings for her and now I'm going to get her to face up to her feelings for me. If that takes seduction, then so be it."

Mitch chuckled. "I'm not sure how you've done it, Beaumont, but you've managed to make seducing one of my best friends sound like the most harmless strategy in the world."

Jay clapped Mitch on the shoulder. "It is, Mitch, my boy. And if you had any sense at all you'd tell Lauren exactly how you feel about her. Then find the nearest bedroom and find out how she really feels about you."

"Good idea. I'll just be going—"

Jay clamped his hand down on Mitch's shoulder. "Not so fast. I need you to help me rig *Osprey* and then we'll take her out on a quick shakedown cruise before I meet Susannah at two."

"A romantic sail. Definitely a key component in any good seduction plan. Can I borrow the boat tomorrow?"

"Only if you climb the mast and rig the headsail," Jay replied.

"Deal," Mitch replied.

"The things we fools do for love of a good woman," Jay said. "It makes me wonder whether this whole love-potion idea really is just a crock."

"I guess we'll find out, won't we?"

Jay turned and stared across the lake. "Yeah, I guess we will."

By one o'clock, Jay was headed across the lake, *Osprey* slicing through the water with the wind at her back. As he came closer to the dock, he noticed a single figure standing at one end, facing the water. As he approached, her features became clearer, and he realized it was Susannah.

She was dressed in a flowing white cotton dress that molded to her figure in the brisk wind. Her hair whipped around her face wildly, freed from a loose braid, and she wore a wide-brimmed straw hat that she held on her head with one hand. God, she was beautiful. His blood suddenly ran hot and he felt himself grow hard as he realized how much he wanted her.

He stood in the cockpit as he maneuvered the boat toward the dock, his eyes fixed on Susannah. It wasn't until he was nearly there that she recognized him and gave him a hesitant wave and a smile. It was all he could do to keep from jumping onto the dock, gathering her into his arms and kissing her senseless. But he fought the urge, and instead deftly lowered the sail and glided the boat along the wooden structure until it drifted to a slow stop. He looped a line around one of the pilings, then hopped out and quickly secured the other lines to cleats on the dock.

She stood at a safe distance, clutching the bottle of champagne watching him, as if she might be afraid to approach. When he finished, he stepped over to her and bent to kiss her lightly on the cheek. He drew his hand along her arm as he pulled away, and realized how young and fragile she seemed without her severe professor clothes.

"I'm sorry about the other day," he murmured. "I had no right to get angry. Am I forgiven?"

She smiled and nodded, then looked over at the boat. "It floats," she said. "You said it would."

"And it sails, as well." He grabbed her hand. "Come on, let's christen her, then take her out for a sail." He felt her pull back and turned to her questioningly.

"I've never been on a sailboat before," she said. "What if I get . . ."

"Sick? Don't worry. We'll just take a short sail to see if you like it, and if you're all right we'll go out farther." He read the hesitation on her face, then reached out and smoothed a line of worry from her brow with his fingertips. Her skin was like sun-warmed silk. "Trust me. You'll love it. And if you don't we'll come right back to the dock."

She nodded again and he helped her on board, then drew her along the deck to the bow of the boat. He grabbed the champagne from her hands and popped the cork. "Would you like to do the honors?" he asked.

Susannah took the bottle. "What am I supposed to do?"

"Usually we crack the bottle against the bow, but I've spent too many hours getting the bow to shine like that and the last thing I want to do is dent the wood. So I guess you can just pour a little bubbly over the prow."

Susannah leaned over the bow pulpit and poured the champagne. It cascaded over the prow and into the water.

"Hold on, there, sailor," Jay said, grabbing the bottle. "Don't waste it all on the fishies." He took a long swig of the warm champagne, then handed the bottle to Susannah with a grin. She followed suit and put the bottle to her lips, then pulled it away, giggling. Her laughter was like the champagne that bubbled over the top of the bottle and ran down her arm.

"If you're going to be a real sailor, you're going to have to learn how to drink like one," he said teasingly. "Now you have to officially say the words. Boats are always christened by beautiful women, so I'll leave this up to you."

Her expression warmed at his compliment. "What do I say?"

He whispered the words into her ear, taking a pause to inhale the fresh scent of her hair before he pulled away.

"I hereby christen this sloop *Osprey*," she said, holding the bottle of champagne high. "May she always find calm seas and strong winds." She paused. "And a good captain to steer her right," she added on her own. With that, she laughed again, tipped the bottle over the prow for the fish, then took another sip of champagne for herself.

It was a perfect beginning to a perfect afternoon. As they sailed, he taught her the mechanics of the boat and was amazed when she was able to describe the physics of the wind on the sails with no help from him. Before long she was helping him trim the sails and steer the boat. He wondered if Susannah would ever stop amazing and delighting him, even after fifty years of life together.

They talked about everything—their childhoods, families, careers, their hopes and aspirations. And sometimes, for long, deep moments, they talked about nothing, just enjoyed a comfortable silence between good friends who somehow sensed they would become lovers soon. The water and the wind seemed to drive all Susannah's insecurities and apprehensions out over the water, and Jay realized that this was the first time that Susannah had ever been truly at ease in his presence.

She explored every nook and cranny of *Osprey*, then sat alone on the prow, her legs dangling over the edge and her toes skimming the water. Later, as she leaned over the bow pulpit and looked out over the water, her dress and unbound hair swirling around her in the wind, Jay drank in the sight of her. He was certain that no matter where he was he would always remember her like this—her face touched by the sun, her skin kissed by the wind.

As the sun began to set over the western shore, the breeze chilled. Susannah returned to the cockpit and Jay bundled her in his jacket, then pulled her back against his chest and wrapped his arm around her shoulders. She relaxed and closed her eyes. Her hands skimmed lightly along his forearm, the simple contact sending jolts of desire to his lap. They both watched as the sun sank slowly toward the horizon.

"I don't want this day to end," he murmured against her temple, pulling her more tightly to him and drawing a deep breath.

"Neither do I," she whispered on a sigh.

She twisted slightly to look up at him and their gazes locked. He lowered his head to taste her sweet mouth. Her lips parted beneath his and he stifled a moan of pleasure. Turning her in his arms, he brought her up against his body until he could feel her soft breasts pressing against his chest. His fingers found their way into her hair and he held her head cradled in his hands as he kissed her slowly and deeply.

Without his hand on the tiller, the boat came about in the wind and he felt it draw to a stop in the water, sails flapping and the boom banging back and forth. But his instincts as a sailor were far outweighed by his desires as a man. He couldn't seem to pull himself away from her soft mouth and grasping fingers.

She clutched the front of his shirt in her hands as if she were holding on to him for dear life, like a woman drowning in her desire. Then, just when he thought she might tear the shirt from his body, her hands slid up to his face. Her fingertips brushed against his cheeks and explored his brow and he broke contact for a moment to place a soft kiss in the palm of her hand.

She stared into his eyes and he saw myriad emotions dance in their depths. She was frightened and unsure, yet he discerned a determination and resolve in her gaze that told him more than words could ever say. She wanted him as much as he wanted her and that realization made his pulse quicken and his blood race.

"It doesn't have to end, Susannah," he murmured, then brushed his lips against hers.

She paused for a long moment and he felt awash in a wave of self-reproach. He had moved too fast; he had pushed too hard. But then she smiled and kissed him lightly.

"No, it doesn't. And I don't want it to."

They put the boat back on course toward the dock at the Canterbury. Somehow that destination seemed the only choice, though the marina and his car were much closer. The rest of the sail passed in silence, punctuated only by stolen kisses and soft sighs.

They tied the boat up at the dock just as the sun slipped beneath the horizon, bathing their approach to the inn in shadows. They walked up the hill, hand in hand, two specters in the warm, peaceful night. As they stepped into the golden spill of light from the veranda Jay turned to Susannah and pulled her into his arms. He rested his chin on the top of her head as he spoke.

"Are you sure about this?" he asked. There was no way he was going to make a mistake with her feelings; there was too much at stake. If she wasn't ready, he wouldn't push her.

"Yes," she replied in a soft but sure voice. "I want you, Jay."

He captured her mouth with his and kissed her, thoroughly, as if to wipe away any traces of doubt she might have left. Then he walked with her up the front steps and through the front door. As he checked in, she stood silently in the corner by the door, her hands twisted in front of her. She looked nervous and dazed at the same time.

He wanted to draw her into his arms and promise her that they would take things slowly. But he could no more vouch for his self-control than she could allay her apprehension. He would simply do his best to make her love him. And to make her see his love for her. The rest he would leave up to whatever passion decreed. And whether their meeting would be explosive or tender, he knew that it would mark a beginning for them, and a commitment to a future together.

Slowly they mounted the stairs to the second floor, her hand clutching his tightly. When they reached the room, he pushed her back against the door and braced his palms on either side of her head. He dipped his head to hers and caught her gaze.

"I love you, Susannah," he said softly, unable, unwilling, to stop the words. "Whatever happens tonight, I want you to know that." He brushed a tendril of hair from her temple and kissed her there, then let his lips drift down her cheek to her mouth. "I love you," he repeated against her lips. "I love you."

SUSANNAH PRESSED her palms onto the smooth surface of the door behind her and closed her eyes as Jay nibbled at a sensitive spot at the base of her throat. He loved her. Her spirit soared and her soul rejoiced. He loved her. Then, suddenly, her knees went weak and her heart dropped in her chest as the true impact of his words struck her.

It was over. Jay had admitted his love for her and the field test was complete. And now it was time to leave him.

She tried to move, but her feet felt glued to the floor. For an instant she panicked at her paralysis, then she realized that her body was making its own decisions—decisions that her brain could not control. She tried in vain to regain her senses, but her mind wandered, focusing on the tiny area of skin that Jay caressed with his mouth, savoring the warmth of his lips, the deep, urgent sound of his breathing.

A moan tore from her throat as he buried his face in the curve of her neck, his beard-roughened cheek rasping against her jaw. She had to stop him! This couldn't go on. But try as she might, her need for him was overwhelming, a sentient force that could not be denied. She wanted him, his body, his soul, his love, if only for one night.

Jay pulled back and fumbled with the key. She held on to his arms, afraid if she let go, her mind would rebel against her body and she would run. After what seemed like an eternity, the key slipped into the lock and the door swung open behind her. Jay tossed the key into the dark room, then pulled her into another mind-numbing kiss.

With tiny steps, they backed into the room. He kicked the door shut with the heel of his deck shoe and it slammed behind them, a shot of sound that startled Susannah into awareness. She nervously pulled out of his embrace and walked to the bedside table to turn on a light. *Leave,* her mind urged. *Run away. Now, while you still have a chance!*

The battle between her conscience and her heart raged on as she frantically weighed the consequences of making love with Jay. But all her noble scientific intentions had mysteriously vanished and she found she had nothing left to fight him with.

To hell with science! For once in her life she wanted to experience love the way others did, with unbridled passion and wild emotion. There were so many questions that begged to be answered. What was beneath the reserved, scientific demeanor of Susannah Hart? Who might she become in the soft magic of this night with Jay? What would he feel like, look like, taste like?

He moved behind her and gently turned her to face him. "Are you all right?" he asked, a look of concern etched across his brow.

She nodded, then reached up and wrapped her arms around his neck. Her kiss was his answer, warm and liquid and filled with all the untried passion yet to come. She would be his and his alone, if only for one night.

Spurred by her ardent reply, he began a tender exploration of her body. His hand massaged the back of her neck, while he cupped her breast in his other hand and rubbed his thumb across the pebbled nipple through the soft cotton of her dress. For a long, languid minute, wild, new sensations pulsed through her body. So perfect, so right, so perfect, so right, her heart thrummed. She surrendered herself fully to his tender ministrations, setting her mind and her conscience free.

His hand drifted from her breast to her waist, then to her buttocks, his fleeting touch leaving her wanting more, so much more. He pulled her hips against his and pressed the swollen evidence of his desire hard against her stomach. A shiver ran through her and she responded by clutching the shoulders of his loose cotton polo shirt in her fists.

His muscles bunched and shifted beneath her hands as he moved to new, unexplored places on her body. He bent down and drew her hard nipple into his mouth through the thin fabric of her dress and bra.

Explosions of desire raced through her and she jumped back as if she'd been burned. Her wide-eyed gaze locked with his, and she rubbed her palms on her hips as a flush of embarrassment crept up her cheeks.

Panic clouded her mind and she stifled another urge to run. Yet this urge was not borne of professional guilt, but of fear of the unknown. She knew nothing of the sensual paths that she and Jay would travel, where his touch might lead her, what pleasures lay hidden around the next bend. She felt like a child, lost and frightened, unsure of the road ahead.

Jay reached out and placed his palm on her cheek. "Don't ever be frightened of me, Susannah. I would never hurt you. I promise."

"I—I know that," she murmured. And she did; deep inside, she felt safe with Jay. With him, she was a woman, not a child. A woman who wanted to know, to feel, the pleasures of a man. And not just any man, but Jay. Jay, who made her feel beautiful and sexy. Jay, who made her feel alive and aware.

With a newborn confidence, she reached out and grabbed the front of his shirt, then pulled it over his head and threw it on the floor beside them. A tightly held breath escaped her lungs as she stared at the smooth, tanned contours of his chest. Hesitantly she reached out to press her palm to his chest. Beneath her fingers, his heart drummed a rapid rhythm.

"Do you feel that?" he asked, covering her hand with his.

She closed her eyes and nodded.

"That's you," he said softly. "That's what you do to me."

Somewhere in the back of her mind, she formulated the correct scientific explanation for his accelerated heart rate, then realized it didn't really make any difference. His desire beat beneath her fingertips and it was real.

He took her hand in his and moved it to his forehead, where she felt a sheen of perspiration dampen her fingertips.

"And this," he said. "Can you feel how you affect me?" She nodded again. Languidly he guided her hand along his chest to the area below his belt. "And this is what you do to me." He pressed her palm into the hard ridge of his erection.

Tentatively she began to stroke him though the fabric of the khaki shorts he wore. Surprised by her boldness, he sucked in his breath and squeezed his eyes closed. His face became a mask of pleasure mixed with pain, as her touch became more aggressive. Suddenly he tensed and a groan rumbled deep in his chest. She snatched her hand away, certain that she had done something wrong.

His eyes opened halfway. "Does it frighten you, this power you have over me?" he murmured, his words tense and urgent.

She shook her head.

He stared at her for a long moment, then smiled crookedly. "Well, it frightens the hell out of me."

She returned his smile as she boldly reached out and began to work his belt open. As if she had opened a door to a new level of intimacy, he moved to unfasten the buttons down the front of her dress. The need between them grew until, in a frenzy, their mouths met and they began to tear at each other's clothing. Gone was the gentle curiosity and the slow, teasing enjoyment, replaced by pure, lust-driven impulse.

Her dress slipped to the floor and she instinctively crossed her arms over her breasts. Her shyness prompted a smile as she felt his lips curl beneath hers. He captured her hands and put them back to work on his belt and loose-fitting shorts. Piece by piece their clothing was discarded, until finally they stood naked, still locked in their endless kiss. Jay turned and guided Susannah along with him, snatching his shorts from the floor before they fell across the bed.

Gently he settled her beneath him. She closed her eyes and luxuriated in the feel of her body pressed along the length of his. He was hard muscle and smooth skin, cool confidence and hot desire, and she wiggled beneath him until he covered every inch of her body like a warm blanket on a cool summer night.

He groaned and tried to hold her still, then gave up and flipped her over on top of him. "That'll teach you," he teased, taking full advantage of her exposed breasts and backside.

She brought her knees alongside his hips and pushed against his chest until she straddled his thighs. Slowly she ran her hands down his chest, then bent to tease at a nipple with her teeth. His rigid penis was hot against her belly as she pressed herself against him, wanting his brand on her skin. "Will you teach me?" she whispered against his skin. Her hair created a curtain around her face, hiding the flush of apprehension that she felt coloring her cheeks.

He brushed her hair away from her face and gave her a questioning frown. "Do you mean you've never —"

She shook her head. "No. I—I mean, yes, I have." She swallowed and forced a smile. "But it was—I didn't know—there wasn't—" She finally gave up and hid her flaming face in her hands.

He pulled her hands away and kissed both her palms, then reached over and fumbled in the back pocket of his shorts. Pressing a small package into her hand, he looked up at her. "Let's start with this," he said.

With shaky hands, she tore the package open. He closed his eyes and his features tensed as she sheathed him. When she drew away, he exhaled and opened his eyes.

Without breaking his intense gaze, he shifted her on top of him until she was above him. He probed at her entrance, and taking his cue, she slowly lowered herself until he filled her completely. The sensation of their joining was exquisitely powerful and Susannah felt the blood drain from her limbs and pool in the moist flesh that surrounded him.

They began to move together, slowly at first and then faster, their pace set by soft urgent moans and quick, shallow breathing. All her thoughts focused on a pin-point of pleasure growing where their bodies were so intimately joined. Instinctively she shifted above him and the pleasure intensified. Though she had never experienced total release with a man before, she was sure that Jay would take her there.

As if he read her mind, his hand moved between their bodies and his fingers urged her on. For a single, shattering moment, she froze, on the edge of a great precipice, and then she felt herself soaring and heard his soft words of encouragement. A vortex of pleasure whirled around her, hot and pulsing, setting every nerve in her body on fire. And then, through the haze, she heard him cry out her name. He joined her there, until their release became complete and they drifted back to reality.

She lay sprawled across his chest, her hair spread over his arm and part of his face. When her breathing had finally returned to normal, she brushed the strands away and looked at him. A tiny glimmer of guilt shot through her as he turned to meet her gaze, but she buried it deep, unwilling to allow anything to spoil what they shared.

"You're a quick study," he murmured sleepily.

She smiled at his sexy compliment. "I had a good teacher," she replied.

"I know," he teased. "The best. And for your dedication to academic improvement, I hereby award Susannah Hart a master's degree in seduction."

She giggled, causing him to slip from inside her. He moaned. "This is serious business. No more laughing."

"Yes, Professor Beaumont," she said in mock compliance. "So now that I have my master's degree, does that mean I'm through with your classes?"

He laughed wickedly and grabbed her around the waist, rolling over until she was pinned beneath him. "Not entirely, Miss Hart," he murmured. He kissed her softly, teasing at her lips with his teeth and tongue. "I was sort of hoping you'd decide to go on for your doctorate."

9

SHE AWOKE from a dreamless sleep as the sun's first rays began to filter through the lace curtains. Susannah lay on her side and stared at the window, confused as to her whereabouts. As she listened to gentle, rhythmic breathing, the significance of her surroundings sank in. She held her breath and waited for the sound to cease, and when it didn't, fragments of the previous night seeped into her mind.

Carefully she raised the elegant coverlet and lace-edged sheets. Oh, God, just as she'd suspected. She was naked. Clutching the edge of the coverlet, she inched her foot back and methodically searched the bed for another occupant. When her foot came in contact with a long, muscular leg, she froze. By now, all recollections of the past ten hours whirled vividly in her mind. There was no sense in denying it, for the damning evidence of her impulsive behavior was right under her nose. Or, to be more precise, under the sole of her right foot.

Susannah painstakingly rolled to her back and pushed herself up on her elbows, taking care not to disturb the warm body that slept next to her. When she had levered herself to a sitting position, she chanced a look at Jay.

He slept, loose limbed, as a child would. One arm was crooked over his head, his face turned into it, and the other rested across his bare chest. She could see only his profile, his strong, compelling features now softened by slumber. She reached out to touch his beard-shadowed face, then stopped herself, clenching her fingers in mid-air. Her gaze drifted along his body, to where the rumpled sheet twisted at his waist, revealing a stretch of bare skin from hip to toe. With infinite care, she pulled the sheet back.

Her breath stopped in her throat as his body was revealed and she stared at the part of him that had driven her to incredible peaks of pleasure just hours before. He was hard, as if he knew in sleep the pleasures that awaited him upon waking. Curious, she reached out and touched him there, her fingertips skimming the silken length of him. Then she pulled her hand away, burned by the heat and the uncontrolled desire that raced through her.

The memories of their lovemaking overwhelmed her, a raging flood of intense responses and passionate murmurs, becoming louder and harsher, mocking her until she felt as if she would suffocate. Biting her bottom lip, she stifled a cry of despair. This was all wrong! She had no right to take the field test this far, to give in to her own selfish wants and needs. She had used him in the worst way and in the process had ruined any chance she might have of putting Jay Beaumont and this whole miserable experiment behind her.

Quaking with suppressed emotion, Susannah slipped out of bed and silently gathered her clothes from the floor. When she was dressed, she stood over him for a long time, staring down at the man who had turned her life, her career, her ambitions, upside down.

"I love you," she whispered, the pain of those words rending her heart in two. Somehow she had known it all along, but had been too stubborn to admit it. Three years of hard work and all her high-minded theories about love and chemistry had come down to one painful realization. Jay Beaumont was in love with her because of her potion. And Susannah was in love with him—in spite of it.

A droplet glistened on Jay's chest and Susannah touched her cheeks to find them wet. She reached out to wipe the tear from his skin. He moved beneath her hand and she drew back, frightened that he would awaken and find her dressed. Backing toward the door, she kept her gaze fixed on him until she felt cool oak against her palms.

"I'm sorry," she murmured as she turned the knob. "I'm so very sorry."

All was silent as she crept down the stairs and out the front door. Though she tried not to look, she couldn't avoid a parting glance at *Osprey*. Through the thin morning mist, she watched the boat rock gently against the pier. She took no pleasure in knowing there would be other breezy afternoons and other women who would enjoy a sail on her gleaming decks.

By the time Susannah made the drive to Science Hall, the struggle to bring her emotions under control had reached a standoff. In between bouts of weeping and periods of bitter self-reproach, she had decided to try to forget about Jay and concentrate solely on her work. Her work would get her through this difficult time. Her work was all she had left.

The building was deserted on an early Sunday morning. Susannah let herself in with her pass key, then made her way directly to her lab. Anxious for the peace and solitude that lab work offered, she wasn't prepared for the company that greeted her.

Lauren was hunched over a microscope as Susannah quietly entered the lab. Startled, Lauren spun to the door and then smiled in relief. "It's you. I didn't expect to see you today." She yawned and rubbed her eyes. "What time is it?"

Susannah hurried across the room and occupied herself with flipping through a stack of file folders. "Seven-thirty, maybe eight," she said over her shoulder. "How long have you been here?"

"All night and most of yesterday. I've been trying to get a handle on the strange effect the potion's been having on Derwin." She yawned again and shook her head to clear it. "That's a pretty dress," Lauren said brightly. "Why are you all dressed up? Are you on your way to church?"

Maybe that wasn't such a bad idea, considering her sinful behavior the night before. Susannah grasped the edge of the counter and closed her eyes, willing the lump of emotion in her throat to disappear. She couldn't give in, not in front of Lauren. "Have you found anything?" she asked.

"Not yet. But I'm conducting a few tests. I should have the results later today. I'm having trouble pinpointing the—"

"I slept with him." The words tumbled from Susannah's mouth and she bit her lip, hoping to stop whatever other confessions were lying in wait. She forced back the tears that threatened and slowly turned to Lauren, preparing herself for an onslaught of questions.

But instead Lauren just smiled. "I knew it!" she cried.

"You don't have to say it," Susannah said bitterly. "I've said it all to myself a million times. Ethically, I should be booted off the faculty. Morally, what I did was reprehensible. I took advantage of the situation. I allowed my own desires to determine my conduct. I broke the cardinal rule of empirical research. I lost my objectivity. I lost my..." She swallowed convulsively. "I lost my..."

A sob broke through her wall of restraint and she buried her face in her hands. "I lost my heart."

She felt Lauren's arm around her shoulders and the tears came harder. "I—I can im-imagine what you must think of—of me," she said through her weeping. "All my—my silly theories about chemistry over emotion. And here I am, blubbering like a lovesick fool over a man I can never have. I'm nothing but a—a fraud, a hypo-crite. A charlatan." She looked up at Lauren through tear-blurred eyes. "I'm sorry."

"Sorry?" Lauren laughed. "For what? For being hu-man? For feeling desire and acting on those feelings? Su-sannah, ever since I've known you, you've held yourself apart from your emotions, as if giving in to them would constitute some kind of failure on your part."

"You don't understand. I'm in love with him," Susan-nah confessed.

Lauren gave her shoulder a squeeze. "I know. I gath-ered that much."

"But he doesn't love me. Not really. Everything he's feeling is coming from the potion. And look at me. I've fallen in love without any chemical inducements, ignor-ing everything I've ever believed in and worked for. I'd call that a pretty monumental failure."

"So you've had a minor setback."

"That's an optimistic assessment of the situation," Susannah replied.

"I'm a naturally optimistic person. You forget, I be-lieve in the magic of love. What are you going to do about Jay?"

Susannah threw her hands into the air and began pac-ing the room, sniffling as she walked. "What can I do? I'll go on with my work. The field test is over. Jay admitted he loved me. We'll present our research and I'll try to forget any of this ever happened."

"I don't think that's what you really want, is it?"

Susannah stopped her pacing. "What I really want doesn't matter. It's just a ridiculous fantasy."

"What do you want, Susannah?"

Wiping at her damp cheeks, she took a deep breath and fixed her gaze on the floor. "I want Jay to love me the real way, without the potion. I want him to look at me, clearheaded and self-aware, and tell me that he still wants me. That he still loves me." She looked over at Lauren. "Pretty hopeless, right?"

"Maybe not," Lauren replied. "Susannah, ever since you told me about Derwin, I've been thinking. There's something not quite right about this formulation. I'm not sure what it is, but I wouldn't give up on Jay until I've had a chance to figure it all out."

Frowning, Susannah tried to catch her lab assistant's lowered gaze. "What is it? Tell me, Lauren, so I can help."

Lauren shook her head. "I'd better work on this on my own. Besides, you won't have much time."

"I have plenty of time now. Especially for my work."

"Not if I know Jay Beaumont. Where did you leave him, in his bed or yours?"

"I left him at the Canterbury Inn, Room 213," Susannah replied, her voice betraying her shame.

"Don't tell me," Lauren teased. "You crept out of bed, gathered your clothes and snuck out of there like a thief in the night. And he never woke up. Am I right?"

Susannah shot her assistant an annoyed glare. "Who are you, the guilt fairy? You're supposed to be my friend. I feel bad enough already."

"Well, I can guarantee Mr. Beaumont isn't feeling so great right now. Men don't take kindly to waking up in an empty bed, especially after they've confessed to the big 'L.' It's a real kick in the old ego."

A wave of panic washed over Susannah. "You don't think he's going to come after me, do you?" she asked. How could she face him, after what she'd done? She'd have to hide out until the potion wore off. That was the only solution.

"I'd lay my best Bunsen burner on it," Lauren replied. "I'll bet he shows up here—" she glanced at her watch "—between nine-thirty and ten—"

Before Lauren could finish the terms of her wager, the door swung open and crashed against the wall. They both spun around to find Jay Beaumont filling the doorway. Susannah instinctively reached for Lauren's hand, then turned to her friend when she couldn't find it.

Lauren grinned, first at Jay and then at Susannah, then handed Susannah a Bunsen burner. "I guess you win," she murmured. "If things get out of hand you can use it for protection. I'll just be going now," she said.

"I think that would be wise," Jay said in a deceptively calm voice. "Dr. Hart and I have a few things to discuss."

Retreating to the far side of the room, Susannah watched her lab assistant leave. The click of the latch sent a shiver of apprehension down her spine and she turned a wide-eyed gaze to Jay.

He returned her gaze with a penetrating stare as he leaned back against the counter and crossed his arms over his chest. After an extended silence, he finally spoke. "Why did you do it, Susannah?" he asked.

She opened her mouth to speak, then snapped it shut. Why *had* she slept with him? Though it seemed like a reasonable decision at the time, she couldn't truly recall what had prompted it in the first place. Lust, love, curiosity, desperation? Or a mixture of all four?

"Answer me! Why did you leave? I thought we had finally decided to face up to what was between us and then you ran out like that."

He wasn't looking for an explanation for the act, she realized, but an explanation for her hasty escape afterward. At least she had an answer for that one. Fear and a huge dose of guilt had sent her running. "I'm sorry," she replied.

"Sorry? Is that all you have to say?"

"I—I made a mistake."

"A mistake." His voice was seething with tightly controlled anger. "How can you call what we shared a mistake? I know what you feel for me, Susannah, and it's far from a mistake."

She shook her head. "No. You don't know. There are things that you don't understand."

"Then why don't you explain them to me."

"I can't," she said, half pleading. "Please, don't ask me."

He pushed away from the counter and slowly walked toward her. "All right, if you won't tell the truth, I guess it's up to me. Let's start with Desirée, shall we?"

Like a punch in the stomach, his words took her breath away. She gasped for air. "You know about Desirée?" she croaked. "But how? When?"

"From the start. Mitch recognized you right away."

"You knew the whole time? Why didn't you say something?"

"Wasn't it clear? I wanted to see how far you'd take your seduction act." He smiled. "Call it scientific curiosity."

Susannah drew a sharp breath. She had an opening here and if she was smart, she would grab it. "All right," she admitted, "now you know about everything. I was doing research on—on male sexual response."

"Oh, yes. I know about everything, Susannah. Desirée, the research . . . your love potion."

She attempted to maintain an outwardly calm facade and forced a casual laugh. "You think I've been working on a love potion? You can't be serious."

His expression tensed. "Don't lie to me, Susannah," he warned.

She stared at him in growing disbelief. This was no bluff. He knew about her potion! "That's impossible! How could you know?"

"It doesn't make any difference," he replied. "The only thing that matters is that it *doesn't* matter. I don't care about the research or the potion or any of it."

His words barely registered, her mind focused on the news that the potion was no longer a secret. What did that mean? She tried to run through the possibilities, but she kept returning to one simple fact. Whether he knew or not didn't really make any difference. The potion had still worked.

"It doesn't change the way I feel about you," he said.

Ignoring the hope that blossomed in her heart, she shook her head resolutely. "Don't you see? You have no idea how you really feel. You're under the influence of a love potion. What you feel isn't real."

He moved to stand before her and grabbed her shoulders. "The hell it isn't. I love you, Susannah. And there isn't a potion in the world that could make me say that if I didn't truly mean it."

Wringing her hands, she avoided his probing stare and searched for a way to explain his feelings to him. "I know what you're going through, but believe me, in time it will pass. The potion has some sort of residual effect, but thankfully it doesn't last long. By my calculations, you should fall out of love with me sometime next weekend, give or take a few days."

"There's no way that's going to happen."

"It will, I assure you."

"It won't. Don't you see how ridiculous this whole thing is? Your potion isn't working, Susannah. The experiment failed and it's about time you admit it."

Her indignation quickly overcame her guilt. "Ridiculous? You're calling my work, my career ridiculous?"

He ground his teeth in frustration. "No, I'm calling the whole idea of a love potion ridiculous. You can't expect me to believe that your potion will magically make people fall in love."

"It *does* work! And I have the research to prove it. Once I've presented my paper, the whole world will accept the fact that love is based purely in chemistry. And that love potions have become a reality."

"Then maybe you can diagram the chemical reaction that made you fall in love with me. I wasn't wearing any potion, so what's your explanation, Dr. Hart. Do we have true love here or just some scientific anomaly?"

She pulled away from him and retreated to the other side of the room. "My feelings have nothing to do with this experiment," she replied.

"But they have everything to do with us."

She clenched her fists and stamped her foot. "There is no us!" she shouted. "Can't you get that through your addled brain? What we have between us is a mirage. It looks real now, but in another week it will just disappear."

"I don't believe that."

"Then believe this," she said, snatching up a file folder from the counter behind her. "Thursday, April 4, no love potion, you consider it luck if I step in front of a bus. Monday, April 14, first application, you show up at my lab without reason and kiss me. April 20, application number two and dinner at the Canturbury Inn, you kiss me again. Tuesday, May 14, we meet at the pool, the potion washes off and you decide you no longer want to see me. Thursday, May 16, you show the first signs of jealousy after another application of the potion. And then there was last night."

"Do go on! I find this fascinating. What about last night?"

She closed the folder and slapped it on the counter. "I doubled the potion's strength and you admitted you loved me."

Jay laughed, then shook his head. "Susannah, there's not a chance in the world that your potion made me say those words. Believe me, I thought long and hard about my feelings for you and I can guarantee, when I told you I loved you, I was of sound mind. And very sound body," he added.

She felt her face flame and turned away. She didn't know whether to be angry or heartbroken. How could he just ignore her work, as if she were simply some crazy scientist with delusions of grandeur? This was her life he was so blithely discounting. She stiffened as he came up behind her and grasped her upper arms.

"I think it's time to face facts," he said softly. "You can't use this potion as an excuse to push me away. Take it from a guy who wrote the book on excuses, it won't work. Admit your feelings, Susannah. Admit that you love me and we'll forget all of this and get on with our life together."

She drew a deep breath and hardened her heart against his gentle urging. "I don't love you," she said, thankful that her back was to him and he couldn't read her expression. "I don't. And it's time you faced *that* fact."

He released her arms and when he spoke, his voice was cold and emotionless. "Fine. If that's the way you want it. Let's just hope you realize your mistake before it's too late."

She turned to him and raised her chin defiantly. "I've made no mistake."

"No? Well, then you go ahead and use your magic potion, Susannah. Use it on as many men as you can. And after you've made them all fall in love with you, I want you to remember who loved you first. And who loved you best."

He grabbed her by the shoulders and kissed her, long and hard. For a moment she lost herself in the sensation of being in his arms again. Then her resolve returned in full force and she shoved against his chest.

"I think you'd better leave," she said softly, trying desperately to keep the emotion from entering her voice.

"That's not what you really want, Susannah."

"Get out," she ordered. "Get out of my lab and out of my life!" She pushed against his chest, but he refused to yield. Tears welled in her eyes and a sob shook her body. "Please," she pleaded. "Leave now."

He reached out to touch her cheek, but she evaded his hand. His expression hardened. "Fine. I'll leave. In fact, I've got a flight back to Baltimore tomorrow morning, so I guess this really is goodbye."

She swallowed her grief and looked up at him with a carefully composed expression, one that was at risk of shattering any moment. "Goodbye, Professor Beaumont."

Jay stared at her, his expression as hard and cold as granite. Then he shrugged and walked to the door. "It's been nice knowing you, Dr. Hart. Have a nice life." With that, he walked out the door and closed it quietly behind him.

Susannah stumbled to a lab stool and sat down, her body shaking and her nerves frayed. Crossing her arms on the counter, she lowered her head and gave in to the weeping that she'd held in check for too long. All her fears and self-doubts came rushing out with the tears. Had she made the right choice, throwing him out of her life as she had? Or should she have given him the time to realize, on his own, that he truly didn't love her? Maybe there was a chance for them. Maybe, after the potion wore off, he would still love her.

She wiped the tears from her cheeks and sat up. No, she had done the right thing. As painful as it was, it would have been more painful to watch his love for her fade and die. At least she could still enjoy the illusion of loving and being loved. She still had her memories of their time together and she knew they would stay with her forever.

Resting her chin on her crossed arms, she stared at Lauren's rack of test tubes. She pulled one out and examined it. To the untrained eye, it looked like water, harmless and not worth a nickel. But she held in her hand a liquid more powerful than any military weapon.

The potion had the ability to alter destiny. To change the course of natural events. To make lovers out of strangers. And she had experienced the full power of the potion firsthand—including the pain and the suffering it could cause to those wanting more than just an illusion of love.

By marketing the potion, she would open the doors to both its use and abuse. Yes, it might save a failing marriage. But it could also be used to destroy a happy one. She slipped the test tube back into the rack and rubbed her tired eyes.

As a scientist, she was charged with objectively studying scientific phenomena and reporting her observations. Of discovering new applications for science and testing them thoroughly. She owed it to the scientific world to release her findings. The potion could help so many.

But would she also be responsible for those it hurt? She pushed the notion from her mind. No, the scientific community would determine the future of her work by their acceptance or rejection of her theories. And once they accepted her potion, they would have to study the possible side effects and weigh the benefits against the drawbacks. She could hardly be held culpable for any future problems.

Susannah laid her head on her arms and closed her eyes, trying to still the wild jumble of thoughts that rattled around in her head. She was so tired. If only she could fall asleep and forget everything—the potion . . . her career . . . Jay Beaumont . . .

A SHARP RAPPING SOUND startled Susannah awake. She looked around the lab, then glanced at her watch. How long had she been asleep? The rapping came again and she stood up.

"Just a minute," she called. She snatched a lab coat from the closet and tugged it on, then walked over to the door. Though she hesitated at first, thinking Derwin, or even worse, Jay, might be on the other side, another loud rap forced her to answer.

Dr. Frederick Curtis pushed past her into the lab in his usual arrogant manner. "Dr. Hart. Miss McMahon told me I could find you here."

"Dr. Curtis. What a pleasant surprise! What brings you here on a Sunday?" Susannah inquired. Dr. Curtis never worked over the weekends. He much preferred the pursuits of the flesh to those academic. Fred Curtis devoted his weekends to the careful study of beautiful and willing women.

He arched his brow. "What are you implying? That I don't put in extra time on weekends?"

"Of course not," she quickly replied. "It's just that it's—"

"I don't have time for chitchat, Dr. Hart," he interrupted. "I'm here because I want an explanation for what's been going on in this lab."

Susannah's heart jumped into her throat. He couldn't know, too, could he? She and Lauren had been so careful. But still, there had been a leak. Maybe, if she was lucky, Dr. Curtis wasn't as well-informed as Jay had been. "Whatever do you mean?" Susannah asked lightly. "We've been working extremely hard on our mud turtle research," she said. "Day and night, in fact. We've had some extremely interesting results from—"

Dr. Curtis held up his hand. "I don't care to hear the insignificant details of your work, Dr. Hart. I simply want to know your intentions."

"My intentions? Regarding what, sir?"

"Regarding Derwin Erwin," he replied.

"Derwin Erwin?"

"Is there an echo in here?" he asked impatiently. "Yes, I said Derwin Erwin. My graduate assistant. Do you plan to marry him? Because if you do, I can guarantee you'll be putting your position at Wisconsin State in severe jeopardy. Though technically Mr. Erwin is not one of your students, he is quite a bit younger than you. I daresay the board of regents will frown upon even the smallest hint of impropriety."

Relief rushed through her. He didn't know! "Dr. Curtis, let me assure you that there is absolutely nothing going on between me and Mr. Erwin. Our relationship is purely professional and anything beyond that is a figment of Mr. Erwin's overactive imagin—"

"Honey bunny, I thought I'd find you here!"

Susannah's heart plummeted from her throat to her feet. No! Why was this happening to her today of all days? She slowly turned around and faced an obviously euphoric Derwin holding a wilted bouquet of daisies and a grocery bag.

"Just as I suspected!" Dr. Curtis said.

"Mr. Erwin, what is this all about?" Susannah asked.

Derwin rushed up to her. "I've decided that I'm not going to wait for your answer, Susannah. You're going to marry me and that's final. Decisions like this are too important to leave to a mere woman, even if she is the future mother of my children. We'll be married by a justice of the peace on our way out of town. I've made a honeymoon reservation for us at the Knotty Pine Motor Lodge on Route 47."

"Mr. Erwin, I am not—"

"They have vibrating beds and cable," Derwin added as a further enticement. "And look, I've bought grape soda and barbecue-flavored potato chips. And I've got my Metalmania tapes in the car, too."

"Derwin, stop this!" she hissed. "I am not going to marry you!"

Derwin turned to Dr. Curtis. "She's just a little nervous about the wedding," Derwin assured him. "You know women. Ruled by their emotions. After we're married, I'll just have to show her who wears the pants in the family."

"I see," Dr. Curtis replied.

Susannah's gaze jumped back and forth between Derwin and Dr. Curtis. "Dr. Curtis, this is not what it... Mr. Erwin, explain to Dr. Curtis that we aren't . . ."

Derwin handed her the flowers. "Sweetie pie, there's no need to explain to Dr. Curtis. I told him everything. How we realized that our passion could not be denied. How you've decided to give up your career to raise our family and take care of me."

Dr. Curtis shook his head disgustedly. "Well, I believe I've heard enough. I certainly didn't expect this from a member of my staff, Dr. Hart. If you know what's good for you, you'll have your letter of resignation on my desk first thing tomorrow morning." He started for the door.

Susannah felt her temper rise. She had had just about enough of these two patronizing fools. "Wait, just one minute, you overbearing, conceited windbag!" she shouted.

Dr. Curtis stopped in his tracks and slowly turned to face her. "What did you say, Dr. Hart?"

"I said—"

"Susannah, I think I've found it!" Lauren's voice joined the fray and Susannah watched her lab assistant rush into the room, her attention fixed on a clipboard. Dr. Curtis spun back around just in time for Lauren to slam into his chest. The test tube she carried slipped from her fingers and shattered at his feet, spraying its contents over the toes of his impeccably polished wing tips.

Lauren stared down at the mess on the floor. "Oops," she said softly. She slowly raised her gaze to Dr. Curtis's angry face. "Big oops," she mouthed as she glanced over at Susannah.

Dr. Curtis directed a withering look at Lauren. Then he glanced down and shook his foot, trying to dislodge the shards of glass that clung to his shoe. "Erwin, get me a paper towel. Now!"

"Yes, sir." Derwin rushed to the sink and pulled a wad of toweling from the dispenser, then hurried across the room and bent over Dr. Curtis's shoes.

A tense silence hung over the lab as they all watched him work. Lauren sidled over to Susannah. "I've figured out the problem," she whispered.

"Problem?" Susannah asked. "And what problem might that be? Right now, I've got quite a number to choose from."

"With the potion. I know what went wrong."

"It's pretty obvious, isn't it?" she mumbled. "Derwin got a whiff and went off the deep end. And now he's taking my career right along with him."

"Just wait a few seconds. If my guess is right, Derwin won't be a problem much longer."

Susannah frowned, then turned to watch a strange scene unfold before her eyes.

As Derwin wiped at the shoes, he leaned closer and closer, until his nose was nearly touching the leather. "These are beautiful shoes, Dr. Curtis," he sighed. "I never noticed how—how handsome they are."

"They'd better be. I paid five hundred dollars for them!"

"Yes, sir," Derwin mumbled. Wadding the paper into a ball, Derwin reluctantly rose from the floor as if in a trance, his gaze still fixed on the shoes. His expression could only be described as enraptured, the same expression Susannah had seen directed at her time and time again.

"Well, Erwin. What are you staring at? I'd better not find any scratches on that leather or I'll—"

"I feel so strange," Derwin said.

"You are strange, Erwin," Dr. Curtis replied, straightening his tie. "It doesn't take a rocket scientist to figure that one out."

"Sir, I think I'm in love." Derwin slowly knelt down in front of Dr. Curtis. Very reverently he touched Dr. Curtis's left shoe. "I must have these shoes, sir," Derwin said, leaning closer to sniff the leather.

"Erwin, get up off the floor!"

Derwin grabbed Dr. Curtis's leg and tried to tug the shoe from his foot. "No. I want these shoes!"

"Let go of me, you sniveling little worm!" Dr. Curtis shook his leg, trying to dislodge Derwin, but Derwin held tight, intent on procuring a brown leather wing tip from his boss's foot.

"I don't love Susannah," Derwin shouted. "I love your shoes. I want your shoes. If I had your shoes, I could be you. I could be powerful. I could sleep with any woman I wanted. I could have a little black book with two-hundred and fifty-six names in it, like you do." Derwin tugged harder. "I could have sex in my office like you did with Denise Linville."

Gasping, Dr. Curtis gave his leg one final shake, then gave up and reached down to peel his assistant away. He grabbed Derwin by the scruff of the neck, yanked him to his feet and steered him toward the door. "I want you out of my sight in ten seconds and out of this building by sundown, Mr. Erwin. I don't know what your problem is, but I would seriously suggest seeking professional help. You are hereby relieved of all your duties as my graduate assistant, effective immediately! There's an assistant's position open with Dr. Flinchbinder. You'll report to him first thing Monday morning."

Derwin's expression was suddenly lucid. "But, sir, you can't mean that! You're assigning me to fungus research? Dr. Flinchbinder's office is in a cave. You remember, we call him Professor Mushroom. Sir, I'd have to watch mold grow."

"Out, Mr. Erwin. Before I personally kick your butt from here to the edge of campus."

Derwin hung his head. "Yes, sir." He gave them all one pitiful last look, including Dr. Curtis's shoes, before he walked out the door.

"I told you," Lauren whispered.

Dr. Curtis cleared his throat and restraightened his already perfect tie. "Professor Hart, Miss McMahon. I'm not sure what went on here today, but I would appreciate your discretion in this matter. We wouldn't want the campus rumormongers to get hold of any unfortunate information. Careers could be ruined over a misunderstanding like this."

Susannah stared after Derwin, another reality of the potion's power striking her. "Yes. Careers were almost ruined, weren't they?" she said softly as she turned back to Dr. Curtis. And what about Derwin and his career? He was an innocent victim of her research and now he was sentenced to an assistantship with a professor who held conversations with fungi.

"Now that we have this problem cleared up, there is no need for your resignation," Dr. Curtis said. "We'll just forget this little incident ever happened, won't we?"

Susannah hesitated for a moment, then smiled. He was worried now. Worried that she'd feed everything she knew about his extramarital love life directly into the campus rumor mill. Maybe there was a way to make everything all right. "I will on one condition, Dr. Curtis," she began. "Actually, make that two conditions."

Her department head narrowed his eyes suspiciously. "Is this blackmail, Dr. Hart?"

"Blackmail? Now, what information could I possibly have to blackmail you with, Dr. Curtis?"

"Ask for a larger research grant," Lauren whispered. "Or a bigger office. And we need a new microscope. Ask for that."

"What is it you want?" Dr. Curtis asked.

"I'll promise to keep your secrets if you'll promise to give Derwin another chance."

"What?" Dr. Curtis and Lauren registered their respective confusion and outrage in a strident duet.

"After three weeks, I want you to give Derwin his job back and forget any of this ever happened. Will you do that?"

"I can't believe you're doing this," Lauren said. "We're finally rid of that little pest and now you want him back?"

Curtis studied Susannah for a long moment, then nodded. "And your second condition?"

"Microscope," Lauren pleaded out loud. "Ask for the microscope."

"I want those shoes," Susannah said.

10

"I CAN'T BELIEVE IT," Lauren moaned. "We could have had a new microscope, and you asked him to give Derwin his job back. Then you asked for his shoes. What could you possibly have been thinking?"

Susannah held the shoes in her hands and examined them closely. "What I really want to know is what Derwin was thinking. Why did he go after Professor Curtis's shoes like that?" The lab grew silent and Susannah raised her gaze from the shoes to Lauren's uneasy expression. "Do you know why he acted so strangely?"

A wavering smile quirked Lauren's lips, but beyond that she looked as though her favorite lab rat had run away. "Susannah, I've got something to tell you. I was going to tell you earlier, but I wasn't really sure of all the facts."

Susannah frowned. Lauren was obviously very upset about something. She put the shoes on the counter and stepped toward her assistant. "What is it?"

"It's about the potion. And Derwin. And Jay."

Susannah's heart twisted in her chest at the mention of his name. Would the pain ever be dulled? "Tell me," she said.

"While I was working on the DNA formulation for Jay, I was also working on a formulation for someone else."

Susannah saw her assistant's distraught state and knew what she was about to confess. "Oh, Lauren. Not Mitch. I'm so sorry."

Lauren shook her head. "No, not Mitch. Derwin."

Susannah gasped. "Derwin? But why would you develop a potion for Derwin?"

"I thought I could use the potion to get him out of the way. I gave what I thought was his formulation to Thelma Pendergrass, the grad assistant in Dr. Norton's lab. I told her it was Derwin's favorite perfume. She's had a crush on the little worm forever, but he's never given her a second look. I thought if he fell in love with Thelma, he'd have something to occupy his time and he'd quit bugging us."

"But he fell in love with me," Susannah said. "Not Thelma."

Lauren winced. "I know. That's because you've been wearing the potion that was formulated for Derwin."

Susannah smiled and shook her head. "That can't be," she said. "You must be mistaken."

"No. I ran some tests on the potion in your vial and it's not the potion we made for Jay. As near as I can figure, Derwin mixed the potions up when he broke into the lab. I tested the three vials left in my rack and they're all filled with Jay's formulation. I retrieved the vial I gave to Thelma and it was filled with the same. Derwin must have switched the stoppers. He deliberately wanted to throw our research off. Susannah, I am so sorry about this. I would have told you sooner, but I wasn't sure. I thought Jay was reacting to the potion just the way we'd predicted and until I could prove otherwise, I—"

"But he was!" Susannah cried. "He was reacting to Derwin's formulation. Just like we thought Derwin was reacting to Jay's formulation. Either way, the potion seems to have a wider effect than we originally anticipated."

"That's not exactly true," Lauren said. "I think you'd better sit down while I explain this."

Susannah pulled out a lab stool and perched on it expectantly.

"There is no way Derwin's formulation could have attracted Jay," Lauren stated.

"Don't be silly. We have the empirical research to disprove that fact."

"I've done some follow-up lab work and I'm certain the potion you used had no effect on Jay. Susannah, I think Jay is really in love with you. Not the potion, Susannah, you."

Susannah's next reply died in her throat and she stared at her assistant, flabbergasted by her revelation. "You're wrong," Susannah said softly.

"I'm right," Lauren countered.

Susannah shook her head. "Look at me, Lauren. Dispassionately, as a research scientist would. Now, tell me, do you really think there's the slightest chance that a man like Jay Beaumont would fall in love with a woman like me?"

"Do you want the truth?" Lauren asked.

"Yes," she replied.

"All right. The truth. I think there's every reason in the world for Jay to love you, but you can't seem to accept that fact. For some reason, you don't believe you're his type. Well, let me set you straight, Susannah. We don't choose who we fall in love with, it just happens."

"It doesn't just happen. It's a combination of genetic imprinting, personal history and pheromones," Susannah insisted.

"That may be. But you had nothing to do with your genetic imprinting. Everyone knows we can't change history. And, as we've seen from this experiment, those little pheromones have an annoying habit of striking off on their own."

"But we've proved our point. The potion works."

"It works all right. But trying to control the reaction is like trying to put out a fire with gasoline." Lauren paused and grabbed Susannah's hands. "There's a fire between you and Jay Beaumont. I saw it earlier. Don't allow it to flicker out and die."

Susannah smiled ruefully. "A fire," she said, pulling her hands from Lauren's and placing them on her flushed face. "Funny, that's how I feel when I'm around him. Like I'm on fire."

"You love him, Susannah."

"Yes, I love him," she replied.

"And he loves you," Lauren said.

She paused and clasped her hands against her breast. Hot tears stung the corners of her eyes. Drawing a deep breath, she said the words that until now had seemed only a dream. "Yes, I do believe he does love me."

Lauren released a long sigh. "Finally. The first bit of common sense I've heard from you since this experiment began. So, what are you going to do about it, Dr. Hart?"

Susannah knew what she had to do. She'd known for some time but had been reluctant to take such a drastic step. Calmly she walked over to the counter, picked up the rack of test tubes that held Jay's potion and stood before the sink. One by one, she removed the stoppers and poured the potion down the drain.

Then she hurried around the room, gathering the files from the potion experiments and placed the stack in Lauren's hands. "Shred these," she ordered.

"What? You want me to destroy our research data?"

Susannah yanked open the top drawer of the file cabinet and stacked more paperwork in Lauren's arms. "Yes. I want you to destroy everything that has to do with the potion research. Every last piece of paper. We aren't leaving here until it's all gone."

"But, Susannah, why? The potion worked! This could be the most significant breakthrough in the study of sexual behaviors this century has seen."

"Well, unfortunately, this century is not going to see it. At least not from me. When you're done shredding those files, come back and get the rest. Anything you have at home, I want you to burn. On Monday morning I want no evidence that our love potion ever existed. Do you understand?"

"The order or the reasoning? Why, Susannah?"

Susannah stopped what she was doing and turned to Lauren. "The potion is power, Lauren. Power that can be misused. Power that can cause pain as easily as it can cause happiness. Believe me, I have firsthand knowledge of this. Besides, people have been falling in love just fine for centuries without the benefit of a love potion."

"But, Susannah, this could bring you the recognition you deserve. You can't throw it all away."

"Yes, I can. I love Jay Beaumont and Jay Beaumont loves me!" Laughter bubbled up from her throat. "And it's just not a good idea to mess with Mother Nature."

Osprey bobbed at her anchor as the passing wake from a motorboat pushed against her hull. The sky above was a perfect blue, broken here and there by a fluffy white cloud. Jay sat on the deck above the cabin, his back against the mast and his Orioles baseball cap pulled low over his eyes.

The gentle rocking lulled him into relaxation, helped along by a bracing fifteen-minute swim in the cold lake and the two beers he'd found in the icebox. He'd been on the lake since early morning, shortly after he'd returned to the Canterbury with the owner's car—the one he borrowed to chase after Susannah.

Jay held his watch up to his face and squinted to read the dial. He had at least another hour before he'd have to head in. Then he'd batten down *Osprey*'s hatches and leave instructions with the marina manager for her care. He wasn't sure when he'd be back to sail her again. Or if he would. When fall rolled around he would have the boat hauled from the water and trucked back to Baltimore, where she would find a welcome home on the Chesapeake the following spring.

Tomorrow morning, he was scheduled for a 10 a.m. flight from Chicago O'Hare to Baltimore. He'd leave Riversbend for a few days to preside over the monthly board meeting of Beaumont Industries and sit in on a navy contract meeting. He was almost tempted to throw all his belongings in the back of the Jag and drive straight through the night, putting Riversbend and Susannah Hart permanently in his past. He'd have just enough time for a shower and shave before the board meeting if he left Riversbend before dark.

But was he really ready to give up? His feelings for Susannah hadn't changed; he still loved her. But a one-sided love affair was the last thing he wanted. He'd played the blindly devoted knight once in the past and he wasn't about to do it again. He wouldn't repeat the mistake he'd made with Cynthia. If Susannah didn't want him, then he would bow out gracefully, with his pride and his ego intact.

He only had one problem. Susannah would be a hard woman to forget. And somehow he knew that the relentless pursuit of other beautiful women wouldn't help. Susannah had been a marker in his life, a road sign that pointed the way to the happiness and fulfillment he'd craved for years.

He didn't want to continue on in the direction he'd been traveling before he'd met her. The bachelor life no longer held any appeal. He wanted to follow a new road with her at his side. He wanted to wake up next to her every day and fall asleep with her wrapped in his arms. And in between dawn and dusk, he wanted to share a lifetime with her, to make a home together and a family.

He stifled a rush of frustration as he realized that his dream might never become real. No matter how hard he tried, he'd never be able to convince Susannah that he really loved her. Not as long as she believed in the success of her love potion. The only hope he held was if the potion failed in further testing. Maybe a year or two years from now, she'd show up at his front door with the news that she had been wrong.

"And maybe *Osprey* will grow wings and fly," he mumbled to himself. Susannah's potion would be a success. Mitch had assured him of her expertise in her chosen field. And Jay had seen her inexhaustible resolve with his own eyes. No, Susannah Hart wouldn't fail at anything she set out to do. She was too damn stubborn.

Jay pushed himself to his feet and winched in the anchor. Then he raised the mainsail and set course for the marina. The peaceful cove he'd spent the afternoon enjoying disappeared behind the stern. He took one look back and tried to catch sight of his property, the ramshackle cabin and the old shed where he'd discovered *Osprey.* He remembered the evening he'd brought Susannah to see his boat. After that evening, he'd realized how much he wanted her. But then the thought of love had been the farthest thing from his mind.

When had it happened? When had he fallen in love with her? Jay tried to think back to the exact moment, but it was impossible. It was as if he'd always loved her; he'd just avoided acknowledging it until the very end. Without a sound, she had edged her way into his heart until she had such a firm foothold, displacing her would be impossible.

As he rounded a point on the northern shore, Jay turned *Osprey*'s bow toward Lake Geneva. He tried to occupy his mind with mentally mapping out the drive to Baltimore. The Tri-State Tollway to the Indiana Toll Road to the Ohio Turnpike to the Pennsylvania Turnpike and then home. Home to his empty mansion on the Chesapeake.

He ran through the route again, hoping to work up some enthusiasm for the trip. It would be good to get back to Baltimore, he assured himself. Maybe there, he could put his life back in order.

SUSANNAH TOUCHED the mascara to her lashes one more time before she reevaluated her appearance in the cocked rearview mirror. Her hair, freed from its usual conservative knot at her nape, curled riotously around her face and over her shoulders. She wore a skintight black knit dress that she had borrowed from Lauren's closet, and underneath, an ensemble of sinfully skimpy lingerie she had purchased just that afternoon at the shopping mall. A pair of seamed silk stockings and black high heels completed an outfit designed specifically for seduction.

Susannah pursed her lips and lowered her lashes. "Hello, my name is Desirée," she said in a throaty whisper. "And I'm here to make all your fantasies come true."

Perfect! The clothes, the voice, the naughty innuendo. How could any man in his right mind resist? Susannah raised her brows and studied her reflection, wondering if Jay Beaumont was in his right mind. After their argument at the lab, she wasn't quite certain that he would welcome a late evening visit from his old pal Desirée.

But all she really needed was to get inside his apartment. Once she was behind closed doors, there was no telling what Desirée might do. And no telling how Jay might react. She pushed open the car door and stepped out into the parking lot in front of Jay's apartment building.

By the time she reached Jay's apartment door, her heart was thundering in her chest and her palms were damp. She knocked softly at the door, then realized that even a man with perfect hearing might miss her summons. Gathering her courage, she rapped harder. Still no answer. She placed her ear against the door and felt the vibration of loud music from inside. It sounded as if he was having a party.

Susannah's heart lurched in her chest. What if he had another woman inside? He'd probably already forgotten her and moved on to someone else. Someone less stubborn and thickheaded. Someone who listened to reason and believed what he told them. She turned away from the door, unwilling to risk the embarrassment of finding some floozy draped across his couch.

Halfway down the hall, she stopped and drew a deep breath. This was her last chance. He was leaving for home the next morning. If she wanted to straighten this whole mess out, she would have to do it now. She spun around and headed back to his door. Banging on it with her fist, she prayed that he would be alone. She'd have a hard enough time dealing with him, never mind an outraged companion.

Finally, after almost thirty seconds of pounding, the door swung open. At first it seemed as if he didn't recognize her. Then his expression brightened and he smiled. He was dressed in a faded T-shirt and a pair of ragged blue jeans. His hair was tousled and his feet were bare. He looked comfortable, approachable and almost happy to see her.

"Are you alone?" she asked.

He grinned. "Not anymore."

"Can I come in?"

"I don't know. The last time you were here you ran out, told me you had to get home to your husband. You stole my hairbrush, too. Maybe I'd better go hide my razor before I let you in."

Susannah reached out and gently placed her palm on his chest. "I promise I won't take anything," she said in a sexy voice. "Unless, of course, it's offered." She felt his heartbeat, slow and steady, beneath her hand.

"What do you want?" he asked, refusing to react to her touch.

She smoothed her palms across his chest, feeling the hard muscle and warm flesh through his soft T-shirt. "What do *you* want?" she countered.

He reached out and touched the thin strap of her dress, skimming his knuckles along her collarbone. Then he twisted a strand of her hair around his index finger and gently pulled her closer.

"I don't want Desirée," he said evenly.

Susannah's heart fell at his rejection and her face warmed with embarrassment. She had been a fool to believe she could ever seduce Jay. What did she know about men, beyond what Jay had taught her in a single night of passion? She only knew what she had read, and according to the books, her appearance should have caused a positive sexual reaction. But, then, research wasn't real life. And Jay Beaumont's behavior never had followed a predictable path.

"I—I'm sorry," she murmured, drawing away from him. "I'll just be going now." She turned to run out the door, but he clamped his fingers around her arm and pulled her back in front of him.

"Not so fast," he said.

"I thought you said you didn't want me," she said, raising her chin stubbornly.

"I don't want Desirée," he replied, looking deeply into her eyes. "I want Susannah."

Susannah bit her bottom lip. She clenched his T-shirt in her fists to steady herself and stared at the Naval Academy logo on the front. "You do?" she breathed, afraid to meet his gaze.

"Always," he said, clasping her hands in his.

"I was wrong about the love potion," she admitted.

"Yes, you were. I know when I'm in love, Susannah. From now on, when I tell you that I love you, I want you to believe it."

She glanced up at him. "Only if you believe that I love you," she said softly.

With that, he dragged her inside and slammed the door behind her. Suddenly she was in his arms. He bent down to cover her mouth with his in a deep, soul-shaking kiss. Then he drew back and looked down at her, smiling. "You are the most stubborn, single-minded . . ." He paused and kissed her again. "Incredibly beautiful, brilliant . . . And you're mine."

Slowly he ran his hands through her hair, twisting its weight through his fingers and raining kisses all over her face. Then his gaze roamed appreciatively over her body, taking in the tight black dress with a bemused look. "Nice dress," he said.

She gave him a wicked smile. So she was right! He wanted Susannah Hart, first and for always. But Jay also possessed a keen appreciation of Desirée. An incredible sense of power came over her. For Jay, she would be both.

She flipped the left strap off her shoulder. "It's really not my style. I borrowed it from Desirée."

He nodded, his eyes fixed on the skin that she revealed. She pushed the other strap down, and his gaze shifted to her right shoulder.

"Personally, I prefer more conservative clothing," Susannah continued. "But Desirée told me men get turned on by a dress like this. Do you?"

"Do I what?" he asked, staring at the cleavage the slipped straps revealed.

"Do you find the dress . . . exciting?" she said, brushing her breasts against his chest.

"Ummm." He bent to kiss her neck and she danced away.

When she stood on the other side of the room, she slowly shimmied the dress down her body and stepped out of it. She heard Jay's sharp breath as he took in her lacy strapless bra and panties and the matching garter belt that held up the silk stockings. Slowly she bent over and picked up the dress. "No," she said, sighing dramatically. "This dress is definitely not my style." She tossed it across the room, where it hit him squarely in the face before it dropped to the floor at his feet.

Jay crossed his arms over his chest and watched her, amused by her little entertainment. "Susannah," he warned. "You'd better be—"

"Call me Desirée," she cooed. She turned her back to him and bent over to unhook a garter, offering him a titillating view of her backside. In one long, delicious movement, she pulled the left stocking down, then walked over to him. "Would you hold this?" she asked as she draped the stocking over his shoulder.

He tried to grab her around the waist, but she deftly avoided his grasp and returned to the opposite side of the room. There she removed the other stocking in the same wanton way. As she straightened, she felt his arms snake around her waist. He pulled her against his body, picking her up off the floor. She screamed playfully and kicked her feet.

"I warned you, Susannah," he said. He shifted her in his arms until she faced him. Squirming in protest, she pressed her hips into his groin and smiled when he groaned in frustration.

"Let me go," she demanded in mock indignation.

"Never," he growled, biting her neck softly. He laid her down on his dining-room table and pulled her legs up until they wrapped around his waist, then buried his face in the curve of her neck, sucking and biting and sending shivers of pleasure down her spine.

As he pushed against her, she heard the crunch of paper underneath her body. She turned her head to the side and found herself staring at a pile of blueprints. "We're ruining your papers," she murmured.

He stood up, desire smoldering in his gaze, his breathing slow and heavy. "Our papers," he said, dipping his head to tease at her nipple through the satin-and-lace scrap of a bra.

"Our papers?" she asked.

"They're plans for our house on the lake," he said distractedly. "God, you taste wonderful."

"Our house?"

He moved to her other nipple and tugged the satin down until his mouth met warm, naked flesh. "Umm, so soft. We'll need somewhere to live after we get married." He stood up and looked at her, his brow furrowed in concern. "You will marry me, won't you?"

Her heart soared as she looked into his eyes, dusky with passion. She reached out and brushed away his worry with her fingertips. "Yes, I'll marry you."

A wide grin broke across his face and he bent down to kiss her gently, this time lingering over her mouth for long seconds. His fingers drifted to her panties and he bent his head to examine her choice of lingerie.

He smiled as his hands skimmed the length of her body, from her knees to her shoulders. "There's just one thing," he said.

"What's that," she murmured, lost in the drenching sensation of his touch, her gaze riveted to his handsome face.

"I may have been a little hasty about getting rid of Desirée. Would you mind if we invited her over for dinner every now and then?"

Susannah laughed. "Dr. Louisa Gruber says that an active fantasy life is an important facet in a successful relationship. In fact, primates often—"

He placed his finger over her lips. "Susannah, this is no time for a lecture on sexual fantasies. I think we'd better do as the doctor ordered and get started on the lab work, because I've got enough fantasies to last us a lifetime."

10th

anniversary

Temptation
is Ten!

Join the festivities as Mills & Boon celebrates Temptation's tenth anniversary in February 1995.

There's a whole host of in-book competitions and special offers with some great prizes to be won—watch this space for more details!

In March, we have a sizzling new mini-series Lost Loves about love lost...love found. And, of course, the Temptation range continues to offer you fun, sensual exciting stories all year round.

After ten tempting years, nobody can resist

Temptation *10th*

anniversary

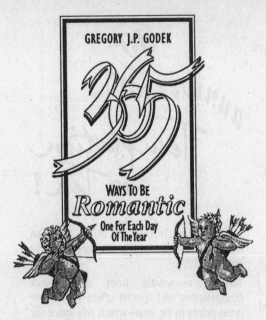
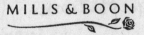

PENNY JORDAN

❧

Cruel Legacy

*One man's untimely death deprives a wife of her
husband, robs a man of his job and offers someone else the chance of a lifetime...*

Suicide — the only way out for Andrew Ryecart,
facing crippling debt. An end to his troubles, but for
those he leaves behind the problems are just
beginning, as the repercussions of this most desperate of acts reach out and touch the lives of six
different people — changing them forever.

Special large-format paperback edition

OCTOBER   **£8.99**

W🌐RLDWIDE

"All it takes is one letter to trigger a romance"

Sealed with a Kiss

Sealed with a Kiss—don't miss this exciting new mini-series every month.

All the stories involve a relationship which develops as a result of a letter being written—we know you'll love these new heart-warming romances.

And to make them easier to identify, all the covers in this series are a passionate pink!

Available now   **Price: £1.90**

MILLS & BOON

This month's
irresistible novels from

AFTERSHOCK by Lynn Michaels

Fire, Wind, Earth, Water—but nothing is more elemental than passion.

Rockie Wexler's father had disappeared, and she needed some help rescuing him. It came in the shape of Leslie Sheridan—but didn't he have reasons for hating the Wexler name?

LOVE POTION No. 9 by Kate Hoffmann

When Susannah invented a love potion, it seemed to work: handsome Jay Beaumont fell in love with her. But she'd never intended to fall in love with him…

ANGEL OF DESIRE by JoAnn Ross

Dreamscape Romance

Rachel Parrish had to stop Shade's quest for vengeance. But she hadn't counted on her very *womanly* response to him. Because Rachel had been heaven-sent with no experience of earthly pleasures…

LOVERBOY by Vicki Lewis Thompson

Luke Bannister, TV's sexiest star, was finally coming home. But childhood sweetheart Meg wasn't going to join his harem. He had dumped her once—she wasn't about to let it happen again!

Spoil yourself next month
with these four novels from

GETTING RID OF BRADLEY by Jennifer Crusie

Since divorcing Bradley, Lucy hadn't had much luck. Her car
had blown up, then her bed! And when sexy cop Zack moved
into her house to protect her, he proved to be even more
dangerous to her equilibrium!

UNDERCURRENT by Lisa Harris

*Fire, Wind, Earth, Water—but nothing is more elemental than
passion.*

When FBI agent Gus Raphael asked Susannah to help him out,
it was the adventure of a lifetime—and her last chance to
convince Gus she was everything he wanted. But was his
becoming her lover all part of the con?

YOU WERE MEANT FOR ME by Elise Title

Emily loved Chris. David loved Liza. But Chris and Liza loved
each other. When Emily and David met at the wedding they
found they had a lot in common. But just when did comfort
and consolation turn into mutual desire?

LOVE, ME by Tiffany White

Chelsea needed a hit song to save her music career—and sexy
songwriter Dakota Law was just the man to write it. But he'd
need persuading… Perhaps she could convince him that she
could fulfil all his wildest desires…and more.

GET 4 BOOKS
AND A MYSTERY GIF[T]

Return the coupon below and we'll send you 4 Temptations absolute[ly]
FREE! We'll even pay the postage and packing for you.

We're making you this offer to introduce you to the benefits [of]
Reader Service: FREE home delivery of brand-new Temptations, [at]
least a month before they are available in the shops, FREE gifts and [a]
monthly Newsletter packed with information.

Accepting these FREE books places you under no obligation to bu[y,]
you may cancel at any time, even after receiving just your fr[ee]
shipment. Simply complete the coupon below and send it to:

HARLEQUIN MILLS & BOON, **FREEPOST**, PO BOX 70, CROYDON CR9 9EL.

- -

Yes, please send me 4 Temptations and a mystery gift
as explained above. Please also reserve a subscription for
me. If I decide to subscribe I shall receive 4 superb new titles
every month for just £7.80* postage and packing free. I understand
that I am under no obligation whatsoever. I may cancel or suspend [my]
subscription at any time simply by writing to you, but the free books a[nd]
gift will be mine to keep in any case.
I am over 18 years of age.

1EP

Ms/Mrs/Miss/Mr _____

Address _____

_____

_____ Postcode _____